ELSPETH MACDONALD would remember her mother's dying words. *Take care of wee Rob. You mustn't let them take him away. You are to stay together. . . . Do you understand . . . ?* Elspeth hadn't understood at the time—who would want to take her brother away? But the meaning of her mother's plea became frighteningly clear when Elspeth learned what their lives as orphans in Scotland would be. A place would be found for her to work as a maid; her little brother would be put in an orphanage.

"We are to stay together," Elspeth had told an unhearing social worker. And they *would* stay together as she had promised her mother. They would run away . . .

*Also by Margaret J. Anderson*

TO NOWHERE AND BACK
IN THE KEEP OF TIME
SEARCHING FOR SHONA
IN THE CIRCLE OF TIME

# The Journey of the Shadow Bairns

## Margaret J. Anderson

Alfred A. Knopf, New York

FOR KATHLEEN BLACK ANDERSON
and the descendants of Arthur and Louisa Black

*This is a Borzoi Book*
*Published by Alfred A. Knopf, Inc.*

Copyright © 1980 by Margaret J. Anderson
All rights reserved under International and Pan-American Copyright Conventions. Published in the United States by Alfred A. Knopf, Inc., New York, and simultaneously in Canada by Random House of Canada Limited, Toronto. Distributed by Random House, Inc., New York
Manufactured in the United States of America.

Jacket painting by Patricia Henderson Lincoln

2   4   6   8   0   9   7   5   3   1

Library of Congress Cataloging in Publication Data
Anderson, Margaret Jean, 1931–
The journey of the shadow bairns.
*Summary:* When her parents die suddenly leaving only a little money and one-way passages to Canada, a young Scottish girl decides she and her four-year-old brother will pursue family plans to relocate.
[1. Brothers and sisters—Fiction.
2. Canada—Fiction]   I. Title. PZ7.A54397Jo
1980   [Fic]   80–12057 ISBN 0–394–84511–0
ISBN 0–394–94511–5 (lib. bdg.)

# Contents

# THE JOURNEY OF
# THE SHADOW BAIRNS

# 1

## "A land of brave and conquering men"

### NOVEMBER, 1902

ELSPETH MACDONALD STOOD BY THE WINDOW STAR-ing out at the slanting rain. When she moved her head, the uneven glass distorted the tall, narrow tenements across the street so that they seemed warped and crooked. She used to think, when they first came to live in Glasgow five years ago, that if she moved her head fast enough the buildings would topple over, letting her see the ocean. Now she knew that beyond these buildings were more buildings, and more beyond that, all the way to the shipyards where Papa worked. Elspeth sighed. Would she never stop missing their Highland home by the sea?

Her thoughts were interrupted by an insistent tug at her worn dress and a plaintive voice asking, "Please, Elspeth. Can't we go to the station to see the trains?"

"For the third time, Robbie—no!" Elspeth said impatiently. "It's too wet."

"But you said you would take me," Robbie persisted.

"It wasn't raining then," Elspeth answered shortly.

"Take him out for a bit—just to play in the close. There's a good lass," their mother said, pulling her chair nearer the meager fire. Elspeth was about to protest, but Mama began to cough again.

Suddenly the room seemed so small and cluttered that Elspeth herself wanted to get outside. "Get your coat on," she told Robbie, taking her own coat from its peg by the door.

Robbie struggled into a gray jacket that was too tight for him and short in the sleeves.

"Wait till I get Pig-Bear ready," he said, looking around the room for the piece of flannel that served Pig-Bear as a coat.

"You're not taking that ragged old animal!" Elspeth said sharply.

"Let Pig-Bear stay with me," Mama broke in quietly, reaching out and taking the stuffed toy from the little boy's hand. Then she adjusted Robbie's cap, pulling it down firmly on his head so that it covered his unruly blond curls.

"Be careful on the stairs!" she called after them as they went out the door together.

Elspeth and Robbie clattered down the worn stone steps of the stairway that they shared with five other families. The stairs were poorly lit and the air was heavy with the damp, sour smells of decay and cats. At the bottom they reached the close, or passageway, which led out to the street. It was here that the tenement children often gathered to play on wet days. Today both the street and the close were deserted, the biting wind and early darkness having driven the other children indoors.

Robbie crouched down in the doorway of the close, collecting a few stones and arranging them in a pattern on the ground. Elspeth watched, wrapping her coat more tightly around her thin body. The way wee Rob could be so oblivious of his surroundings and amuse himself with so little always filled her with a mixture of irritation and admiration. He could find as much to interest him in a Glasgow gutter as she had found at his age in the clear waters of the Morvan Burn that ran through their farm into Loch Nevis. But then, he had been born in Glasgow and had lived all his four years in one room in a tenement building. He had never known the croft on Loch Nevis that she and Mama and Papa had left behind five years before.

Elspeth had been only eight then, but the little stone house, with the mountains rising steeply behind and the waves breaking on the white sands out front, was still sharp in her mind. She remembered the rich smell of the slow-burning peat in the fireplace, and the vivid purple of the heather on the hill, and the cry of the curlew on the moor. Despite the wild beauty, Papa had not been able to make a living on their few acres of heath and bog and rock, and so they had come to Glasgow. Papa had found a job in the shipyards, hoping to earn enough money to buy medicine for Mama and someday to move back to a farm again. But here they were, five years later, still crowded in one room, with walls so thin that they could hear the neighbors' shouting and arguing. And Mama was no better. If anything, the cough was worse, and lately she tired even more easily.

A thin gray cat sidled into the doorway, and Robbie immediately abandoned his game with the stones to stroke the animal. It was as starved for affection as it was for food and responded by purring loudly, arching its back, and rubbing against his leg. Elspeth, meantime, was idly watching a lone figure who had turned the corner onto their street, shoulders hunched and head bent against the driving rain.

"It's Papa!" she said to Robbie. "Here's Papa! I wonder why he's home so early."

Robbie immediately forgot the cat. Unmindful of the rain, he and Elspeth ran to meet their father.

"What are you bairns doing outside on a day like this?" Papa asked, drawing Robbie under the flap of his coat. "You'll catch your death of cold, the pair of you. Come on home with you!" But he was glad of their welcome.

"You're early, Papa," Elspeth said, looking up at him, her wide gray eyes anxious. "There's nothing wrong, is there?"

"Not a thing!" answered Papa. "It's good news I'm bringing. And pies for supper!"

He handed Elspeth the bag he was carrying. Elspeth smiled at him, reassured. Something exciting must have happened, right enough, for him to be bringing hot pies home from the bakers and it not even payday!

It wasn't until after supper was eaten and the table

cleared that Papa finally told them his news. Pulling a pamphlet from his pocket, he spread it out on the table and asked, "How would you like to go to Canada and take up farming again, Margaret?"

"Canada!" Mama repeated quietly. "But how would we pay for it?"

"I've got a bit put by," said Papa. "And the land is free. Just imagine! A hundred and sixty acres of good farmland, and all we have to do to make it ours is to live there on it for three years."

"But we'd need a house to live in," said Mama.

"We'll build it ourselves. And we'll have help in getting started. This man—the Reverend Isaac Moses Barr—has already obtained land along the North Saskatchewan River from the Canadian government, and he wants to take a group of settlers out there. He'll arrange for supplies and for tents till we get houses built, and he'll see to it that there are roads and churches and schools for the children."

"But, Duncan, it's so far away," said Mama, shaking her head slowly. Her hair fell forward over her thin face, hiding the bleak expression in her eyes.

"We have Donald and Maud out there," Papa said encouragingly. "It will be good to see Donald again and find out how things are going."

"He could have written," said Mama.

"Maud sent us that letter from Manitoba. Donald's likely too busy to write, with all those acres to farm."

Papa didn't say—as he might have done—that the main reason that Donald did not write was because it would be too much effort. Neither Papa nor his brother Donald had had much chance to go to school when they were children living on a remote farm in the Highlands. Papa often said that the best thing about coming to Glasgow had been that Elspeth had learned reading and writing and arithmetic, and that soon Rob, too, would go to school.

"When would we go?" Mama asked, and then was shaken by a bout of coughing.

"Early in the spring so that we can get a crop in the first year," answered Papa. "They say that the sun always shines there, even in winter. You'll feel so much better away from the rain and damp of Scotland, Margaret. It's that as much as anything that makes me think we should go."

Elspeth's eyes were bright with excitement as she listened to every word Papa said. To be back on a farm again, Mama well, Papa doing the kind of work he wanted to do, their own home, their own land, maybe a dog for wee Rob. . . .

As if reading her thoughts, Rob climbed onto Papa's knee and asked, "Can I have a dog when we get to the farm?"

"We'll need a dog on the farm right enough, to chase the cows over all these acres," Papa answered.

"But can it be *my* dog?" Robbie persisted.

"Maybe it will, or maybe you'll have a calf of your own. Elspeth used to have a calf up on the croft by Loch Nevis."

"And do you remember Fleecy?" Mama asked with a smile. "That great sheep that thought she was one of the family?"

"I raised Fleecy from a newborn lamb," Elspeth told Robbie. "She lived in the kitchen when she was little, and she never did take to the outdoors or to the other sheep."

"Do you remember how she liked it when we sang 'Bonny Doon'?" Mama said, humming a few bars of the melody.

It was good to hear Mama sing again. She must like the idea of Canada, Elspeth thought.

"I'd rather have a calf than a sheep," Robbie declared. "Then I'll get milk. A wee calf called Jock!"

"You'll not get much milk from a calf called Jock," Elspeth said with a burst of laughter, and even Mama and Papa joined in.

Robbie, who didn't like being laughed at, especially by Elspeth, turned red and his lower lip trembled.

Papa came quickly to his defense. "Rob's going to make a fine farmer. He's good with animals, and he accepts what happens and makes the best of it. You need to be able to do that in farming. You, Elspeth, would sooner bend things to your own way."

"And isn't that what *you've* done, Papa?" Elspeth challenged. "You didn't just accept losing the croft, or we wouldn't be talking about going to Canada now."

"Maybe so," Papa agreed. "But then, I've worked for this. It has taken time and planning. Here, lass, read us some of what Isaac Barr says in this bit paper of his."

Elspeth looked at the pamphlet that her father handed her. There were lots of big words and flowery phrases describing the advantages of the settlement that Barr was proposing. Her eye lighted on one paragraph near the end. Clearing her throat, she began to read hesitantly, but as she read her voice gained in confidence.

" 'I do not desire to present a picture that is highly rose-colored. There are difficulties and drawbacks to be encountered; but for the brave man obstacles are something to be overcome and steppingstones to victory and success. Let me say, in brief, you cannot pick up nuggets of gold on the surface of the soil; you must dig for the wealth of the land. Hard work and plenty of it lies before you, more or less of hardship, and not seldom privations. You must sometimes sweat, and sometimes you must suffer from the cold. If you are afraid, stay at home—don't come to Canada. It is a land of brave and conquering men.' "

As she read the last words she looked at Papa with a shining face. A land for the brave!

# 2

## "Sometimes you must suffer"

### MARCH, 1903

THE MACDONALDS HAD NO PROPERTY TO DISPOSE OF, no relatives to worry about, and very few possessions to pack; and so they gave their time to dreaming and planning—and it was mostly dreaming, because they had little foundation for planning. Elspeth read Mr. Barr's pamphlets all the way through. The promises of blue skies and broad fields of rippling golden grain pierced the drabness of the cold, wet winter evenings. Papa told boisterous stories of the days when he and Donald were lads on the farm, and Mama sang songs that Elspeth had not heard her sing since they had lived on the croft.

On the third day of March, running home from school, Elspeth felt a new warmth in the sun and a softness in the breeze that spoke of the coming of spring, although there were no trees or flowers on their street to mark the changing of the seasons. Elspeth no longer noticed the confining gray buildings. In less than a month she would be on her way to Canada, the land of sunshine and green, fertile plains.

In school that day Miss Johnstone had been talking about Canada. She had shown them pictures of lakes as big as the ocean and a tremendous waterfall called Niagara Falls. Elspeth clattered up the stone stairs eager to tell Mama all about it, but when she opened the door she was shocked to find that the room was full of people—neighbors she scarcely knew, all talking together in hushed tones but with an undercurrent of excitement in their voices. They fell silent when they saw her in the doorway. Elspeth wanted to turn and run away, but instead she had to listen to Mrs. Copeland from across the stair saying awful things—things that couldn't be true. Papa had been hurt at the shipyards . . . falling scaffolding . . . he wouldn't get better . . . Mama had gone to see him. . . .

Then Mama came home, and Elspeth knew that all that Mrs. Copeland had said was true—and more. Papa was dead. Mama's face was shriveled, and her eyes had lost their luster the way seashells do when they lie forgotten on a dusty shelf. She had no words of comfort for Elspeth, and Elspeth had none for her. The neighbors brought them supper, but only wee Rob ate.

Papa was buried in St. Andrew's churchyard. Mrs. Copeland minded Robbie while Elspeth and her mother went with a small group of mourners to the cemetery. The hint of spring of a few days earlier was gone. Rain fell steadily from slate-gray skies. Gusts of wind, funneling between the church and a high stone wall, snatched away the words of the minister.

But no words could have soothed Elspeth as she watched her father's coffin lowered into that barren ground—so far from the heathered hill behind the croft and the fertile soil of Canada with all its promises.

Mama came home from the funeral chilled and weak. The cough that had plagued her all winter was much worse, and she didn't seem to have the strength to care what would happen to them now. When Elspeth tried to ask her, she turned away. So Elspeth kept Robbie quiet and made meals that her mother could not eat. She kept asking Mama if she should fetch the doctor, and Mama finally gave in and told her to bring him.

When the doctor came, he listened to Mama's chest and then told Elspeth that he was going to take her mother to the hospital. Elspeth had thought that Robbie was hardly aware of what was happening, but now he clung to Mama, not wanting her to go away.

"We'll make your ma better," the doctor promised Robbie, prying his fingers loose from the bedclothes. Turning to Elspeth, he said, "You can help by looking after your little brother."

"Aye, take care of wee Rob," Mama whispered hoarsely. "You mustn't let them take him away."

"I won't," agreed Elspeth, not knowing who would want to take him.

Her mother seemed to sense that Elspeth did not understand. Struggling, she raised herself on her elbow and said feverishly, "Don't let them take him.

You are to stay together. Do you understand me?"

"I'll look after him, I promise," Elspeth said. After all, she was quite used to minding Rob while their mother was sick. She had done it many times before.

One evening, a week later, the doctor came to the door. He was the same doctor who had promised Robbie he'd make Mama better. In halting words he told them that Mama had died. "Do you have any relatives?" he asked.

"There's Uncle Donald and Aunt Maud," Elspeth whispered. She did not say that they lived in Canada. She did not tell him that she didn't have their address.

During the week that followed, Elspeth was numb with grief and resentment. Perhaps if she had cried, the neighbors who came to see them, sometimes bringing them meals and shaking their heads and clucking over "the poor orphan bairns," would have understood her better. But she scowled at them wordlessly, her face pale and pinched, her eyes dry. She brooded over the unfairness of it all.

Robbie cried and whined constantly, wanting Mama and Papa. He couldn't seem to realize that they were dead. Elspeth was angry with him for still hoping that they would come back and everything would be all right again. Yet she, too, listened for Papa's footsteps on the stairs and wakened in the night wondering if Mama needed her. Each morning, when she first woke up, she struggled to escape from the sorrow that had invaded her dreams, only to find that it was in her waking life too. She understood now why Mama hadn't wanted to talk about what would happen to them. Elspeth no longer cared either.

After the initial rush of sympathy from neighbors, no one knew what to do about them. Someone finally called in a social worker. She came to the house late one afternoon, a stiff-starched woman, and told Elspeth that a place had been found for her to work as a maid. She said that Robbie would have to go to an orphanage.

"I had thought you would be bigger," the woman said, looking down disapprovingly at Elspeth. "They told me you were fourteen."

"Thirteen, ma'am," said Elspeth.

The woman studied Elspeth standing in the middle of the room with Rob beside her. Even for thirteen she was small and slight, and her coarse brown wool dress hung loose in all the wrong places, making her look smaller. Her mouse-brown hair was pulled back from her forehead, sharpening her narrow face. Her thick-lashed, wide gray eyes looked dull and defeated.

"I wish you were stronger-looking," the woman said. "But if you're a willing worker, then I'm sure they'll take you. It's a live-in position, so that solves a lot of problems for you."

"We are to stay together," Elspeth said, reaching out and taking Robbie by the hand.

The woman now looked at Robbie properly for the first time and saw a dirty child in ill-fitting clothes. He was chewing on the ear of a battered stuffed animal and his nose was running, but he looked up with trusting blue eyes. His tousled hair was blond and curly, and his face still had its baby roundness.

"I know of someone who might give a home to your little brother—Robert, is it?" the woman said, with a touch of interest in her voice. "It would be better for him than the orphanage. You're a good boy, are you?"

Robbie nodded.

"We're to stay together," said Elspeth more firmly.

"How old is he?" the woman asked, ignoring Elspeth.

"He's four, ma'am."

"They really want a baby . . . but maybe I can talk them into taking a four-year-old," she said, looking Rob over as if he were a stray puppy. Then she consulted her watch and added briskly, "I can't do anything more until Monday. Can you stay here over the weekend? I'll get Mrs. Copeland from across the way to look in on you from time to time."

"We'll be all right, thank you," said Elspeth.

Elspeth waited tensely until the woman left, afraid that she might change her mind and take Robbie with her. The clipped sound of the woman's heels echoed on the stone staircase and then faded away as she hurried out to the street.

"She's one of *them*," Elspeth said quietly to Rob. "One of *them* that Mama said would want to separate us. She wants to take you away, but I'm not going to let her. We'll run away before she comes back."

Elspeth forced herself to sit down and think calmly about what she was going to do. She wanted to get away at once, before anyone else came to see them, but it would take more planning than that. It would also take money. Papa had kept his savings in a tin box at the back of the dresser, but only he ever opened it. Surely it would be all right for her to look inside?

She found the tin box, but still she hesitated. Robbie was watching her curiously. "It's all right, Robbie," she said. "It's ours now." Elspeth opened the box and groped inside with shaking fingers. It seemed to be full of pamphlets and papers and letters. Impatiently she scattered these, finding at last the pile of money—far more than she dared to expect. Slowly she counted it—almost a hundred pounds.

They could go a long way on a hundred pounds, maybe even take a train somewhere. But where would be the best place to go? They could go back to the croft in the Highlands. Some of Elspeth's feeling of hopelessness began to dissolve as she pictured the little stone house by the edge of the sea, with the mountains rising steeply behind. Robbie would like it there—the sea and the sand and the lambs in the spring. . . .

As she shuffled through the papers, looking for an envelope big enough to hold the money, she noticed the pamphlet that Papa had asked her to read. She shoved it to the bottom of the pile because it hurt too

much to remember. And these were surely tickets—
tickets for the journey Papa would never take. Tears
ran down Elspeth's cheeks.

"I'm hungry," cried Robbie. "I want my tea."

Elspeth did not answer. She was staring through
tears at the blurred words on the tickets: *The Lake
Manitoba, Beaver Line*. Was that the name of a boat?
But Manitoba was where Uncle Donald and Aunt
Maud went. Would the boat go there? Could they go
to this place called Manitoba and find Uncle Donald
and Aunt Maud?

She studied the tickets again more carefully: *March
31, 1903, Liverpool Dock*. This was Friday, March
27—three weeks since Papa . . . . She pressed her
hands against her temples, trying to force her
thoughts back to the words on the tickets.

"I'm hungry," Robbie said again, twisting his
finger in his hair as he often did when he was upset.

Elspeth ignored him. These were boat tickets, and
there were others that seemed to be train tickets, but
for a Canadian train. How were they to get to Liverpool to go on the boat? Once again she sorted through
the papers, but still she could find no train tickets from
Glasgow to Liverpool. Then it occurred to her that
they could go to the train station and buy tickets.

It was five years since Elspeth had traveled by
train, but she was familiar with the routine of the
station because of the many hours she had spent there
with Rob. Going to see the trains was his favorite
outing. He had once gone to the station alone, and

Mama had always worried that one day he would take it into his head to climb on board a train. Sometimes they pretended they were travelers bound for far-away places with exciting names like London and Carlisle and Liverpool—and now it could really happen! Wait till Robbie found out!

"Elspeth!"

Reluctantly, she put aside the tickets and stirred up the fire, moving the kettle onto the stove. While she waited for it to boil, she spread bacon drippings on two thick slices of bread and then put them on plates on the table.

"Wait till I get the tea made," she told Robbie, who had started to eat.

After supper, Robbie climbed into bed and quickly fell asleep. Elspeth went back to her planning.

They would need to take their clothes with them, and maybe blankets too. She dragged Papa's battered traveling bag out from under the bed. It was made of soft leather, scarred from many journeys, and was hinged at the back so that it opened into two halves, separated by a partition. She put Rob's few extra clothes in one side, and hers in the other. She packed two towels, tin plates, mugs, and a knife, fork, and spoon for each of them.

Sadly she looked at the familiar things they would have to leave behind—the blue porcelain plate that had come with them from the croft, the old china doll that her mother had played with as a child, the dark picture of a stag standing in front of heather-clad hills. She would take Mama's brooch, a cairngorm surrounded by a wreath of silver thistles, and Papa's watch for Robbie. And the money. How should she carry all that money?

Suddenly she had an idea. She found the sewing needle on the corner of the mantelpiece where Mama had always kept it, then took out her old gray skirt with the lined bodice. Sitting in Mama's chair by the window, where there was more light, she painstakingly began to unpick the seams. Then she stuffed bundles of pound notes between the lining and the bodice, stitching them in place so that each bundle was secure. She bit off the thread with her small, even teeth. There, that would keep the money safe. And maybe she wouldn't look so small and skinny now, she thought, smiling slightly to herself.

She put on the skirt and bodice and pulled her brown dress over it. Then she crossed the room and shoved the suitcase back under the bed just in case that old busybody Mrs. Copeland should come in and ask questions. She paused, looking down fondly at Robbie. His tousled hair was red-gold on the pillow, and he was holding Pig-Bear in the crook of his arm. She tucked the blanket under his chin and hoped that he would sleep until morning. He had taken to waking in the night, crying. Bad dreams, she supposed. She had bad dreams too, but there was no use *her* crying.

Elspeth planned to leave the house early on Monday morning before that woman came back. They'd catch a train to Liverpool and hide there until it was time to get on the boat on Tuesday. She thought of leaving right away, but Mrs. Copeland might tell someone they were gone, and Elspeth didn't know where she could hide with Robbie. He was hard enough to look after here, crying all the time, and wanting Mama. She felt guilty about being so impatient with him. She didn't mean to be.

For much of the day on Saturday, Elspeth stood anxiously by the window watching the people down on the street. Suppose the woman didn't wait till Monday to come back? Suppose she had already talked to the people who might want Robbie, and they came and took him away? Her fingers tightened on the windowsill. She leaned forward to watch a woman approach their doorway. Elspeth sighed with relief when the woman continued down the street and disappeared into the cobbler's shop.

"Can we go and see the trains?" Robbie asked, pulling at Elspeth's dress.

"Not just now," she answered. She would have liked to tell him about the plan, but he might say something to Mrs. Copeland.

"I want to go now," Robbie wailed.

"Then want must be your master," Elspeth answered sharply. Then, realizing that Mama used to say that, she pulled Robbie toward her and held him close. Was it easier, or harder, being only four? she wondered.

Elspeth felt a little calmer on Sunday morning, but a loud knock at the door brought back her earlier panic. She opened it cautiously and didn't know whether to be relieved or upset when she saw Mrs. Copeland standing there, her inquisitive eyes raking the whole room. Mrs. Copeland was one of those people who savored other people's misfortunes.

"So they've found you a place as a kitchen maid," she said, shuffling over to Mama's chair and sitting down as if she meant to stay for a while. "I remember my first job as a kitchen maid. At everybody's beck and call, I was. And all those copper pots and pans to be shined up every day."

Robbie leaned against Mrs. Copeland's knee and she ruffled his hair, saying "Poor fatherless bairn! That so much could happen in three short weeks! I was standing right by the door when the man from the shipyard came to tell your ma the news."

Her voice was like a probe opening up a wound. Elspeth crossed to the window and stared down at the street. There was nothing to distract her, not a person in sight.

"Oh, well! I just came over to help you pack your bags," Mrs. Copeland finally said, getting heavily out of the chair. "Do you have a bag for the lad's clothes?"

"I've got everything ready," Elspeth answered firmly.

"Aren't you taking the pretty plate and the doll—something to remember your dear mother by?"

"I'll pack those later. We can manage on our own."

"Well, I'll go then," Mrs. Copeland said, moving slowly to the door. "But I'll look in early in the morning to see that you're ready. You don't want to keep the lady waiting, do you?"

That night Elspeth hardly slept. She sat in her mother's chair by the window, watching for the first sign of dawn. For the first time since Papa's death she felt a faint stirring of anticipation. She and Robbie were going to Canada! They would find Uncle Donald, and they would make Papa's dream come true.

It was not yet light, but Elspeth shook Robbie awake. He whimpered and wriggled down under his blanket.

"Wake up, Robbie! Wake up! We're going to the station."

Rob's blue eyes flew open. "To see the trains?" he asked.

"To go in a train," she answered.

Robbie looked up at Elspeth, trying to guess if this was a game she was playing. She hadn't played games for a long time. Her serious face told him nothing, but he allowed her to stuff him into two jerseys and button up his coat, and then tie his bundled-up blanket on his back without complaining. He didn't even remind her that they hadn't had breakfast when she cautiously opened the door and led him out of the room he had lived in all his life and down the dark stairs.

# 3

## "Difficulties"

### MARCH 30

WITH THEIR BUNDLES ON THEIR BACKS, ROBBIE AND Elspeth walked hand in hand down the deserted street. A dog bounded out of a doorway and sniffed at Robbie, who would gladly have stopped and patted it if Elspeth had not pulled him away.

"Come on, Robbie," she urged. "We'll have plenty of time to play when we get to the station. But we must get there quickly."

The traveling bag was awkward to carry. It was so big that Elspeth had to crook her elbow slightly to keep it off the ground and her arm was becoming tired. Robbie was dragging on the other hand.

"Here, change hands," she said to him.

"You carry Pig-Bear," he whined.

"I can't. I'll put him in the bag."

"No! He has to see!"

Elspeth knew better than to argue with Robbie about Pig-Bear, but all the same, she felt that Pig-Bear was a responsibility she could have done without.

When they reached the windy entrance to the

station, Robbie ran ahead, excited by the sounds of shunting trains and the sooty smell of the engines. Dim light filtered through the smoky glass roof, and Elspeth was glad to see that, even at this early hour, there were lots of people about. She and Robbie would be less conspicuous that way.

First they went to the tearoom. Robbie was wide-eyed with surprise when Elspeth sat him down at one of the tables and ordered two thick mugs of tea and two buns. Robbie had often peered into the tearoom on their visits to the station, but had long since learned that no amount of begging would persuade Elspeth to take him in there. Today he could not understand his good fortune as he bit into the big flat bun.

After breakfast they went to the rest room. It was hard to drag the case and blankets everywhere, but Elspeth didn't dare leave them unguarded.

"Robbie, you'll have to stay with our things while I go in here," she told him, sitting him down firmly with their bundles in the outer waiting room.

She was gone only a few minutes, but when she returned the bag and two blanket rolls were lying there alone. Robbie was nowhere in sight. The glass door out to the station was swinging slightly. Hoping that he had just left, Elspeth pushed her way through the door, colliding with a fat woman carrying two suitcases. When she was out in the station Elspeth looked frantically up and down. There was no sign of Robbie. The feelings of tension that had knotted her stomach all morning gave way to panic.

A shrill whistle announced the arrival of a train at Platform 10. Elspeth ran wildly through the station, hoping that she would find Robbie standing by the ticket barrier watching the train come in. When he wasn't there, she imagined that he had somehow gotten past the barrier and onto the platform. Doors banged open and porters rushed forward with clattering trolleys. Rumpled, sleep-stained passengers tumbled out of the train and surged toward the ticket collector's gate, but there was no sign of Robbie.

"Please, sir, please, sir," Elspeth said breathlessly. "Did you see a little boy with blond hair, sort of curly, go onto the platform?"

"Stand back," said the ticket collector impatiently, not even listening.

"Please, sir," she began again, but the first people had reached the gate and the man gave all his attention to punching tickets.

Elspeth turned and walked back toward the waiting room wondering what she should do. A policeman in a heavy dark coat and helmet was coming through the station entrance. He would help her— but the thought that he might ask questions held her back. Suppose Mrs. Copeland had told someone they had run away, and the policeman was looking for them.

Elspeth forced herself to be calm. Robbie had to be somewhere in the station—he never would go home until he had seen a dozen trains come and go. He couldn't have been on Platform 10 because the bad-tempered ticket collector wouldn't have let him pass. She decided to search each of the other platforms in turn.

She was almost back to the waiting room again before she spotted him, sitting against a wall on a stool, talking to a shoeshine boy.

When he saw Elspeth, he waved. "Jock let me shine my shoes!" he said happily.

Elspeth didn't need to be told that. Robbie's worn brown boots were generously covered with black polish, as were his face and hands.

"Robbie! I told you to stay with our stuff," said Elspeth, tears of annoyance mixing with tears of relief. "We've got to get back there and see that no one has taken it."

"Want your shoes shined, miss?" the shoeshine boy asked impudently.

"Did you have to let him get in this mess?" Elspeth replied angrily.

"Hope he doesn't catch it when his ma sees him," answered the boy.

Elspeth turned quickly away to hide that awful pain of missing Mama. She couldn't allow herself to think of that now, so she jerked Robbie to his feet and dragged him back to the waiting room.

"Pig-Bear!" he shouted. "I've left Pig-Bear!"

They had to go back for Pig-Bear. His feet had been lavishly dipped in shoe polish—one black and one brown—so that he was now more disreputable than ever.

When they finally got to the waiting room the

bundles were undisturbed, much to Elspeth's relief.

"Now can we go and see the trains?" Robbie wanted to know, but Elspeth wasn't ready for that yet. She was still trembling from the fright Robbie had given her. Somehow she had to impress on him the need to stay together and not draw attention to themselves.

"The trains," said Robbie.

"In a wee while," Elspeth promised. "But I'm going to tell you a story first."

Rob's face brightened. Except for watching the trains, Rob liked nothing better than listening to Elspeth tell stories, but he had almost given up asking for a story. She hadn't told him one for weeks.

"About Pig-Bear?" he asked.

"It's about Pig-Bear," she nodded. "And these two bairns. It's a kind of game they're playing."

*Bairns*. That had been what Papa had always called his children. Elspeth sat down on a bench, her feet propped up on their precious luggage, and wee Robbie snuggled up beside her.

"These bairns—Elspeth and Robbie—are going to have a big adventure."

"And Pig-Bear too," Robbie reminded her.

"And Pig-Bear too. They're going on a train, and maybe they sleep on the train. It takes them to a place called Liverpool. Then they go on a boat—a great big boat—and they eat on the boat and sleep on the boat. After a long time the boat crosses the ocean and gets to Canada, to this place called Manitoba, where they find their Aunt Maud and Uncle Donald."

"Do they go on the train soon?"

"Yes, but listen carefully. There's another part to the story. These bairns—Robbie and Elspeth and Pig-Bear—have to be very careful on the journey, and *very* quiet. Above all, they *must* stay together. The little bairn, Robbie, mustn't run off by himself like he did this morning."

"Or Pig-Bear," said Rob sternly. "He stayed with Jock when he should have come with us." He gave Pig-Bear a slap to remind him to be obedient.

"You see," continued Elspeth. "There are people who don't want these bairns and Pig-Bear to go on this long journey. They might try to send them back—and you do want to go, don't you?"

Robbie nodded solemnly.

"If you want to get there, then you must stay quiet and hide in the shadows. You see, we don't always know who it is that's going to try to stop us. We mustn't let *them* get us."

Robbie looked around nervously at the other people in the waiting room and snuggled closer to Elspeth.

"We'll play that we're Shadow Bairns," she said. "And we must always stay together and keep quiet."

"Shadow Bairns," Robbie whispered.

Elspeth smiled, satisfied that she'd found a way to keep him quiet whenever she needed to, but the words left a lonely echo in her mind. She saw herself and Robbie always alone, hiding in the shadows, not really knowing where they were going. But it would be a far worse loneliness if she let them take Rob away from her. And she had promised Mama. Jumping up, she said loudly, "Come on, Robbie! We'll get you cleaned up."

After she had washed Robbie, she took him to see the trains. Sometimes he forgot about being a Shadow Bairn, shouting with excitement and running ahead of Elspeth, who was always hampered by the luggage. Mostly, though, he stayed near her, watching the commotion and bustle of the station. Elspeth studied the board that announced the train departures. *Liverpool: 11:25 from Platform 4.*

At eleven o'clock, Elspeth said to Rob, "You stay here with Pig-Bear and the luggage. I'm going to buy the tickets—you can watch from here."

Robbie nodded. "We're Shadow Bairns minding the luggage."

Elspeth went over to the ticket counter, sure that Robbie would stay where he was now that it was part of a game. She pushed two crumpled notes through the grille, saying, "One and a half to Liverpool, please." She had decided not to risk asking for two children's tickets in case the man remembered that later if people were looking for two runaway children.

"Singles or returns?" he asked, not even looking up from his tickets.

"Singles," said Elspeth.

He smoothed out the notes and put them in the drawer, pushing the tickets and a handful of change toward her. He never looked up. She put the tickets carefully in her pocket and then went and bought food for the journey with the change—warm mutton pies, buns, and apples. They shared a pie while they waited for the train.

When the train arrived at Platform 4, giving out impatient snorts of steam, Robbie pushed forward, but Elspeth held him back. They mustn't be noticed and remembered. She looked over the people crowding toward the ticket barrier and saw a mother and father, each carrying a child, followed by two other children clutching the mother's skirts. Dragging the suitcase, Elspeth got in behind them and told Rob to stay close.

She gave the man their tickets, and as he punched them and handed them back, she heard him mutter, "It'll be a long journey wi' all them bairns!" He had taken Rob and Elspeth to be part of the family!

With a surge of confidence, Elspeth and Robbie headed toward the first empty carriage and were scrambling aboard when a porter asked, "Are you children traveling First Class? Where's your ma or pa?"

"They're looking after the luggage," Elspeth lied. "They told us to get on the train."

"Can I see your tickets before you get in there? Or does your pa have them?"

"Here they are," Elspeth said, showing him the tickets.

"Third Class! I thought as much. Come along!"

He took them farther down the train to an empty compartment, saying, "Sit there by the window, and I'll see if I can find your pa."

"Maybe we'd better find another seat," Elspeth said, watching the porter heading toward the luggage van. "He might come back and start asking questions."

"We're to stay here," Robbie protested. "He's gone to look for Papa. He said he'd find Papa."

"Oh, Robbie!" Elspeth said in an exasperated voice. "You know he won't find Papa! He's likely one of *them* that will stop us from going to Canada and Uncle Donald."

Robbie winced at Elspeth's words, almost as if she had struck him, and followed without a word when she led the way down the corridor to another compartment. He climbed onto the seat and sat very close to her, twirling a curl of hair with his forefinger and sucking on Pig-Bear's ear. His eyes never left the door, but whether he was waiting for the porter or Papa he did not say.

"The train's starting soon," Elspeth said at last. "You can sit next to the window so you can see better."

Robbie seemed to forget his grief and fears when the train pulled out of the station. He flattened his nose against the window, watching houses and bigger buildings flash past, and then farms, fields of cows, sheep on the hillsides, and occasional towns. It was a whole new world for Robbie, who had never been outside Glasgow before. Elspeth wished that she could forget her worries as easily. The way Robbie still expected Mama and Papa to come back bothered her. He was usually so quick at grasping ideas. Look at the way he had understood about their being Shadow Bairns. She could tell from the way he was sitting so close to her, and so quiet, that he was still a Shadow Bairn. So why did he force her to say over and over again that Mama and Papa weren't coming back?

These thoughts were interrupted when the train stopped at a small station and a man and woman came into the compartment. The woman was tall and sharp-faced; the man was short, with very blue eyes and thin, sandy hair. It took them a long time to get settled because they had so much luggage, and the woman was very particular about what pieces could go up on the rack.

"Not that one, Jim," she said in a flat voice as her husband tried to lift a wooden crate. "That's got the china in it."

Elspeth looked at the label on the crate—*Beattie, Lake Manitoba, Canada*. So *they* were on their way to Canada too. Elspeth looked at them with interest.

When at last the luggage had been arranged to the woman's satisfaction, Elspeth braced herself for the questions she was sure would come. She was going to say that Uncle Donald and Aunt Maud had sent for them to come out to Canada. But the woman paid no attention to them, fixing her gaze a little above Elspeth's head. After a while Elspeth craned her neck to see what was so interesting up there. She saw a picture of the Tower of London. How strange that the woman would gaze at it for an hour when there was so much to see outside. The man half smiled in

Robbie's direction once or twice, but didn't speak to them either.

Elspeth turned her attention back to the window and watched the countryside sliding past. They came to another station—Carlisle—and here the platform was crowded. The train stopped with a jerk, and Elspeth found herself staring at a family grouped on the other side of the glass. The father was a big man, tall and blond, and his wife had reddish hair, escaping in wispy curls from under a flat black hat. A boy of around fourteen, blond like his father, was rounding up the luggage, and two little girls, both with stubby red pigtails, were clinging to two elderly women. The two women were apparently not going with the family, for they were hugging and kissing the little girls and crying quite unashamedly. The father and son lifted the cases into the train. The family paused outside Elspeth's compartment, but seeing the amount of luggage on the racks and floor, they didn't come in.

Elspeth watched them pass with a sudden wave of longing for her own mama and papa. If only it could have been the way they had planned it. Papa had not been one to talk much about his hopes, but Elspeth knew how he had longed to get away from the city, back to the land again. A piece of land of his own that would one day pass to his children—that had been the dream that had sustained him through all the long hours he worked in the shipyard. Now it was up to her to make the dream come true.

Papa had said you could have a hundred and sixty

acres of land free, just for living on it for three years. Of course, they might not let her have it because she was so young, and a girl, but she would worry about that later. Aunt Maud and Uncle Donald would help her. She didn't know how she was going to find them, but she'd worry about that later too.

"Do you hear what it's saying?" Robbie asked suddenly, breaking into her thoughts.

"What who's saying?" Elspeth asked.

"The train," Robbie answered. "Listen! It's saying, 'They won't catch us! They won't catch us!' "

Elspeth gave Robbie a quick hug, and he smiled up at her. They snuggled together. Lulled by the rhythm of the train, Robbie fell asleep. Soon Elspeth slept too, worn out by the tensions of the weekend.

# "Steppingstones to victory"

## MARCH 31

THEY SLEPT THAT NIGHT ON THE TRAIN, WHICH HAD been shunted into a siding near Liverpool Station because there was nowhere else for the passengers to go. Every hotel and boardinghouse within miles was full.

The following morning, the two children joined the vast crowds hurrying from all parts of the city toward the dock where the *Lake Manitoba* waited. There was no need to ask the way. Elspeth could hardly believe that so many people could all be going to Canada.

About the time the children joined the throng pushing toward the gangplanks, the Reverend Isaac Moses Barr was looking down from the vantage point of the deck of the *Lake Manitoba*. Seeing the crowds below, he felt like Moses of old, leading his people to the Promised Land. He didn't look like Moses, for he was stocky, and clean shaven except for a small moustache that drooped over the corners of his mouth. He peered nearsightedly through round spectacles that were misting over in the light rain.

Around his neck was a clerical collar, and on his head a white cap.

Isaac Barr wasn't worrying about how to squeeze more than two thousand people into a boat equipped for less than eight hundred, nor how to feed them in dining rooms that wouldn't accommodate a quarter their number. He scarcely noticed the mountains of luggage still piling up on the dock. Instead he was congratulating himself that he was giving so many people a chance to escape the smoky industrial cities of England. He was strengthening the ties between Britain and Canada. He smiled complacently at the thought that he was changing the course of history.

These exalted thoughts were interrupted by a nervous young man in the uniform of a head steward. "Mr. Barr, sir! There's too many people wanting to come on board, sir. There's more than we have beds and bedding for."

"Then they will have to share bunks or sleep on the floor."

"Some of the stewards have deserted the ship, sir. They're afraid, sir. There's too many people."

"Then hire more stewards from among the passengers," Mr. Barr answered impatiently. "That will solve both problems—more stewards and fewer passengers."

The young man was bewildered. Surely Mr. Barr must be joking, but there was no hint of a smile on Barr's broad face as he looked down at the waiting crowd.

"They're still coming," said the steward.

"Aye, they're still coming," echoed Barr. "And there is a great land waiting for them—a great fertile land under the dome of God's own sky. Have you seen the cities these people come from—their horizons limited by the walls of factories and tenement buildings, the sky stained black with smoke belching from a hundred chimneys?"

Mr. Barr's voice rose and fell as if he were talking from a pulpit. The steward shuffled nervously, waiting for a chance to interrupt.

"This immigration scheme will be a pattern for other people to follow," Mr. Barr went on. "We're changing lives. You're seeing history being made."

"But what about all these people, sir?"

"Let them come on board."

The gangplanks were lowered and people pushed forward, each one determined to have a place on the ship. There had been rumors circulating all morning that Barr had sold more passages than the boat could hold. One look at the waiting crowds seemed to confirm this.

Elspeth could feel the surge of movement when the first passengers were allowed on the ship somewhere far ahead. She was surrounded by tall men in heavy coats, smelling of wet wool and tobacco. The suitcase was hard to manage, and she worried about getting separated from Robbie. He was having his own troubles, being continually shoved aside and buffeted by suitcases and hampers.

As they were pushed nearer the ship, Elspeth tried to plan what she would say to the ticket collector. It should be easy to convince him that she and Rob had been separated from their parents in this crush, but how was she to find out where they should go on the boat? Was she supposed to have tickets for rooms or beds? She looked up at the side of the ship, rising above the dock like a great white wall. Was it like a train inside, with lots of seats?

Her worries were interrupted by a small but urgent request from Robbie.

"Robbie, you've got to wait!" said Elspeth, desperately looking at the mob of people hemming them in.

"I can't wait," said Robbie tearfully.

"It won't be long now," Elspeth lied, knowing that it could well be hours before they were on the boat.

"I can't wait!" said Robbie again, and promptly wet his blue serge trousers.

Right then, Elspeth decided that running away had been a mistake. There were more problems than she could cope with. When she got on the boat she'd tell the ticket collector that they were by themselves. Let *him* worry about Rob's wet trousers. With that decision made, it was easier to wait her turn to board the *Lake Manitoba*.

They were squashed tighter now, so tight that Elspeth could not even look down at her own feet, but she eventually felt the edge of the gangplank and shuffled forward and up. The traveling bag caught on a ridge of board nailed crosswise on the ramp. She felt the pressure of the crowd behind her as she struggled to free it. The handle was slipping from her grasp, but she managed to jerk the bag up. "Hang on to me, Robbie!" she shouted, but her words were lost, muffled by the crush of bodies around her.

At last they were on the deck. Elspeth looked wildly around for Robbie, only to find that he was right beside her, flushed and tousled, but much less worried and frightened than she was. There was no sign of any official looking at tickets, so Elspeth and Robbie joined the crowd pouring down the stairway. When they saw some other children, they instinctively followed them, and found that all families with children were lodged together in the middle hold.

Elspeth felt vaguely disappointed that the boat wasn't more like the train. There the seats had been covered in soft red velvet and the little lamp fixtures had been gold. Here everything was of raw wood and bare boards, as if it were still being built. The hold was partitioned off by upright posts. Boards nailed to these formed crude bunks, sometimes two deep, sometimes three. Instead of mattresses there was loose straw, and the floor was covered with sawdust.

The hold was a huge room, dimly lit by paraffin lamps. As more and more people crowded in, it seemed smaller and became unbearably hot and noisy. People were claiming bunks, spreading their belongings around, shouting at their children. Tentatively, Elspeth set their bundles on a bottom bunk, but a woman immediately told her to move along because that bunk was taken.

In the far corner, Elspeth spotted a narrow opening between the bunks on the end wall and those on the side. Wriggling into it, she found that the ends of the two sets of bunks and the side of the ship formed a space like a tiny room. Pulling Robbie in beside her, she whispered, "This is where the Shadow Bairns are going to live."

Robbie liked their corner. Right away he began to build Pig-Bear a castle out of the sawdust on the floor. Elspeth filched some straw from neighboring bunks, just in case they had to sleep there on the floor. She hoped that once everyone was settled she would be able to claim a leftover bunk without causing any fuss, but the way people were still pouring in there weren't going to be any bunks left. Already arguments and even fights were breaking out. People were being forced to give up some of the bunks they had claimed and put two or three children in one bed.

Elspeth spread their blankets and sorted out their clothes. She helped Robbie change his trousers, laying aside the wet ones until she could find out where to wash them. Getting on the boat now seemed so easy that she was ready to cope again. She wouldn't tell anyone they were alone—not yet. After all, she had even thought of bringing along a bar of yellow laundry soap.

The bunks on either side were occupied now, but no one paid any attention to them. One woman hung blankets over the end of her bunks, which made their corner very dark.

"Pig-Bear can't see," Robbie complained. "And I'm too hot. I want a drink of water."

"I'll get you a drink soon," Elspeth promised,

wondering what they were going to do about meals. She was beginning to realize there was a lot she didn't know. "We'll go back up and take a look around, but you're to stay right beside me."

"Like a Shadow Bairn," Robbie said, nodding solemnly.

They crawled out of their corner and made their way through the crowded hold. The first flight of stairs was more like a ladder than a staircase. They had to push their way between people who were still on their way down. Two more flights brought them to the deck.

It was a relief to be outside. A thin drizzle of rain was falling, but the day seemed bright in contrast to the gloom below. They stood in a sheltered place between a lifeboat and the rail, absorbed in the bustling activity all around them. Passengers still hurried up the gangplanks, cranes swung precarious loads of luggage from the dock to the hold, and a mob of gulls was fighting over a basket of bread that had burst open on the dock. The smell of the sea, the wet salt wind, and the cries of the birds reminded Elspeth of their faraway home in the Highlands. For a moment, even she who had so little to leave behind suffered a pang of homesickness, but that was forgotten when a straggling band assembled on the dock played "God be with you till we meet again."

"They're singing to us!" Robbie said, jumping up and down with excitement and clapping his hands.

The pulse of the engines and the shudder of the boat drowned out the last quavering notes. A cheer went up from those staying on the shore, answered by a louder cheer from the deck. When the ship pulled away and the people on the dock were just a dark blur, all waving white handkerchiefs, Robbie was still waving back. He thought that everyone was saying good-bye to him.

Elspeth watched the receding shore. *They* couldn't get Robbie now. She put her arm protectively around his shoulders, pulling him closer to her. If only Mama and Papa could be here too. She tried to shake off the black feeling of loneliness that slipped over her when she thought of her parents. She turned to Robbie. "We've done it, Robbie! We ran away and no one stopped us!" But somewhere in her mind came the answering thought—no one really cared. Abruptly, Elspeth turned her back on England and pulled Robbie over to the stairs.

At the bottom of the first flight they passed a dining room where a steward was setting out a tub of ship biscuits and another of hard-boiled eggs. As soon as his back was turned, Elspeth dashed forward and shoved four eggs into her pockets. She took a biscuit for each of them.

"Was it all right to take them?" Robbie asked nervously when Elspeth divided the spoils back in the hold. "Won't they be angry?"

"It's our supper. It's meant for us," Elspeth reassured him. "It's just better to eat it here by ourselves. I'll take our mugs and fetch tea, but you wait here."

The ship biscuit was about six inches across and an

inch thick, so it kept Robbie quiet for a long time. For both of them an egg was a rare treat, and they'd never had two each before.

By evening, Rob and Elspeth knew their way around the ship. They heard plenty of angry complaints about the crowded holds and makeshift washrooms, but they thought nothing of it because they had shared a toilet with five other families back in Glasgow.

Robbie didn't want to sleep, with all the excitement and noise. On one side of them a baby was crying. On the other, a man and his wife were arguing.

"I'll lie down here right beside you," Elspeth said, tucking a blanket around Robbie. "Look, here's Pig-Bear!"

The quarreling voices became still, and they could hear the mother singing softly to her crying baby. Tears filled Elspeth's eyes as she recognized the sweet, sad music of "Bonny Doon," a song that Mama used to sing. "Ye mind me of departed joys, departed never to return." Elspeth began to cry.

Robbie reached up and touched Elspeth's wet cheek. "Don't cry, Elspeth!" he said softly. "*They'll* never find us here. *They* won't know where to look."

She snuggled closer to him. Was it easier or harder for Robbie, not being burdened with so many memories? she wondered. As time went by, he would forget Mama and Papa. But at least he still had her, and she had him. Comforted by this thought, she finally drifted off to sleep to the soothing sound of hymns.

For the first time since Mama had died, Robbie slept through the night. They were awakened by the sounds of the families around them beginning their second day at sea. Elspeth went to wash a few clothes in a scant bucket of water one of the stewards had provided, leaving Robbie behind. When she returned to the hold she was surprised to find that he was not alone. Two freckle-faced girls stared up at Elspeth. They both had fine, light-red hair, almost orange, twisted into tight braids. They looked about eight or nine years old. Elspeth was sure she had seen them before.

"They're Rachel and Rebecca," Robbie said eagerly. "They want to be Shadow Bairns."

"Shadow Bairns are quiet," Elspeth said sternly. "How do they know about Shadow Bairns if *you* were quiet?"

"Pig-Bear went out and that one—Rachel—found him. I had to go out and get him. Shadow Bairns stick together."

Elspeth looked at the girls and wondered how Robbie knew which one was Rachel. They looked exactly alike. Then she remembered where she had seen them before. At Carlisle Station, with their father and mother and brother, saying good-bye to the old ladies.

"Please, will you let us be Shadow Bairns?" Rebecca asked.

"Let them," Robbie pleaded.

Elspeth looked at his eager face. It might help to have friends on the boat, even though they were younger than she was. And playing with them would keep Robbie amused. "All right," she said.

"I knew she'd let us! I knew she would!" Rachel said to Robbie.

"But first you have to show that you know *how* to be Shadow Bairns. You have to creep through the hold and up to the deck and hide behind the lifeboat near the top of the stairs without your brother seeing you."

"How do you know about our brother?" Rebecca asked.

"Elspeth knows everything," Robbie answered proudly. "I'll show you the lifeboat."

Elspeth watched them go, looking forward to a few minutes to herself. Robbie and the twins merged with the shadows, passing through the hold with exaggerated caution, but no one paid any attention to them. It was easy to be a Shadow Bairn! Easy to go unnoticed, even in a place where there wasn't enough room for everyone. Elspeth suddenly found that she didn't want to be alone after all. Taking the clothes she had just washed, she followed the children to the deck, giving them time to reach the lifeboat first.

They had pulled a piece of loose canvas around them to shut out the wind, and were sitting together, snug in its shelter.

"We did it! We did it!" shouted one of the twins.

"Shadow Bairns are quiet," Elspeth reminded her.

"Tell us more about Shadow Bairns."

Elspeth sat down beside them and told them about this place called Manitoba where the Shadow Bairns were going. She could see the place clearly just from the sound of its name. It was a small town, with steep mountains behind, close to a huge lake, like the picture Miss Johnstone had shown them. The houses were white, crowded close together, and had steep red roofs and doors of different colors.

"What color is Uncle Donald's door?" Robbie asked.

"Blue," Elspeth answered. "Blue like the water in the lake. And all around the lake are beaches of silver sand."

The story was interrupted by an angry shout. "So that's where you brats are hiding! I should throw you overboard, because that's where Papa and Mama think you are by now, and I'm getting the blame for it! You come back down to your bunk and stay there!"

"We can't, Matthew! We're Shadow Bairns," said Rachel.

"We weren't to tell," shouted Rebecca.

The boy grabbed the twins and pulled them toward the stairs, both of them yelling loudly.

"Maybe their brother wants to be a Shadow Bairn too," Robbie suggested when they were gone.

Elspeth shook her head. He was too old to pretend things like that. Besides, he hadn't even noticed her and Robbie.

"I'm hungry," Robbie said.

"Maybe there are still some eggs and biscuits," Elspeth answered hopefully. "Let's go down to the dining room."

The stewards were bringing in pots of stew and mashed potatoes. Elspeth and Robbie hesitated in the doorway, drawn by the warm smell of the food, but afraid to go into the crowded dining room.

"Have your ma and pa lost their appetites already?" a friendly steward asked. "Come on in and help yourselves."

They filled their bowls and sat close together at one of the big tables, eating quickly and feeling like uninvited guests at a party. The benches were nailed to the floor, and the tables had raised edges that made it difficult for Robbie to reach his food. They soon understood the reason for the raised edges when bowls and mugs slid across the table as the ship rolled.

"Hold on to your dish, Rob," Elspeth warned. Too late. Robbie's plate had shot across the table.

"One bowl of this muck is enough for me!" said the man opposite, pushing it back.

Robbie laughed, and they both began to feel more at ease.

After dinner they went down to the hold. The mother was singing to her baby, and someone was snoring loudly on the other side. Their dark corner now seemed familiar and welcoming. A feeling of well-being settled over Elspeth. She and Robbie were together, part of this huge family of people, all going to Canada.

# 5

## "If you are afraid"

### APRIL 4

EARLY THE FOLLOWING MORNING, THE RED-HEADED twins crawled into Elspeth and Robbie's corner. "It's all right! We *can* be Shadow Bairns!" said one of them.

"And Matthew says he'll be *them* and look for us," added the other.

"But you weren't to tell anyone!" said Elspeth. "You haven't even kept the first rule."

Before she could say more, Matthew peered through the narrow entrance. "This is a great hiding place," he said. "Though it's a bit small. I don't think I can get in."

"Nobody asked you," Elspeth answered sharply.

"What's this about Shadow Bairns? And getting up to the deck without me seeing you?"

"It was just something to do," Elspeth answered guardedly.

"I bet you couldn't make it around the boat without me seeing you—not if I was looking for you!"

"I'm sure I could," said Elspeth.

From that beginning, Shadow Bairns evolved into a game far more complicated than hide-and-seek. It was played all over the ship, with Matthew usually the seeker. The game went on for days, and the longer they played, the more refined and complex the rules became. For Robbie and the twins, the line between make-believe and reality became blurred. They crept about like Shadow Bairns all the time, hiding and whispering together. For Elspeth, it was just a game, but she had never had the freedom to play like this before, and so she enjoyed it as much as any of them. Playing with Matthew and his sisters drove away the loneliness, the feeling of not belonging. She grew more and more daring, looking for new places to hide. There was hardly an inch of the ship the children did not explore.

It was on the fifth day of the voyage that Elspeth climbed to the forbidden First Class deck in response to a dare from Matthew. The wind was strong, blowing salt spray that stung her face and bare hands. On such a wild afternoon the deck was deserted, so she was not particularly careful, and almost bumped into a man standing alone in a corner somewhat protected from the wind. He looked like one of the crew because he was wearing a white cap, but Elspeth noticed he also had a stiff white minister's collar. He bowed slightly, and introduced himself as Isaac Barr.

Elspeth stared at him, completely overwhelmed to find herself in the presence of the leader of the whole expedition. This was the man they had talked about in Glasgow, the man who had written the pamphlet Papa had asked her to read.

"I hope things go well for you and your family in Canada," he was saying earnestly.

Elspeth nodded dumbly.

"It's a big responsibility, you know," he continued. "Taking all you people to the New Land—but you'll find a better life there."

Elspeth looked up at him. He hadn't even noticed that she was too poor and untidy to be on the First Class deck. His thick round glasses hid the expression in his eyes, but Elspeth thought that he looked sad. How awful to have to worry about *all* these people. At least she was only responsible for Robbie.

"It's people like you we need on this venture," he continued. "Young, willing to learn, to adapt."

Suddenly Elspeth knew that here was someone who would really understand why she and Robbie had come by themselves. They weren't just running away from the social worker. They were going to make a new life for themselves. They wanted to see the Promised Land. He would know how to find Uncle Donald and Aunt Maud. But before she could say anything a steward appeared on the deck. One glance at his outraged face told her that *he* could see that she didn't belong there. She turned and ran.

On her way down to the hold she met Matthew, who asked her where she had been.

"Up on the First Class deck," she answered, trying to sound casual, but unable to keep the triumph out of her voice.

"You were not!"

"I've been talking to Mr. Barr."

"I don't believe you!"

"I was so!"

"I wouldn't waste my time talking to him any-way," said Matthew. "Papa says he's crooked."

"He is not! Don't you know that he's the one who organized all this?"

"That's what I mean! Look how we're crowded in here. But I didn't come to argue with you. I've been looking for you all afternoon because Robbie's sick. He needs you."

Elspeth didn't wait to hear more. She stumbled down the steep steps in her hurry to reach the hold. The air was thick with the smell of smoke and sickness and stale food. Rob lay listless on his blanket, worn out by vomiting. Elspeth tried to reassure herself. Lots of people were seasick, and the boat was pitching more than ever. But as the afternoon wore on, Robbie became worse. Tears ran down his pale face, and time and again he called out for Mama.

"Hush, Robbie," Elspeth said, looking anxiously out from their corner through the narrow opening. She was afraid that Robbie's crying would attract attention, but at the same time she wished that someone would come and tell her what to do.

"Do you want a drink of water?" she asked, holding a mug to his lips.

The water only made him sick again.

Night came, and Elspeth crouched beside Robbie,

his head resting on her lap. She listened to the creaking and groaning of the boat as it protested the wild tossing of the sea. The lamps in the hold had all been extinguished, but here and there people had lit their own candles, which formed small pools of flickering light. Elspeth's corner was completely dark, so that she could not see Robbie. Sometimes he was frighteningly quiet and at other times loud and demanding. He constantly asked if *they* were near, and mumbled about being a Shadow Bairn. Elspeth wished that she had never invented the game, yet she found herself reminding him that Shadow Bairns were quiet when he called out too loudly.

The boat rolled more violently. A suitcase crashed from an upper bunk and the baby was crying again; nearby, someone was moaning. Elspeth's head ached from lack of air and lack of sleep. Her leg was numb, but she didn't want to move in case she disturbed Robbie. She stroked his damp, sticky forehead and wished that Mama was with them. She would know what to do for him. "Take care of wee Rob. Don't let them take him. You are to stay together," Mama had said. But this wasn't what Mama had meant. She wouldn't have wanted them to run away. Elspeth felt cut off from the past, cut off from the future. She tried to imagine them arriving at Uncle Donald's and Aunt Maud's house, the cousins running out to meet them. But the crying baby and groaning passengers drove such comforting thoughts from her mind.

Morning brought little change. The storm still raged, and the hold was dark. Robbie was quieter now, but Elspeth knew that she must get help. She thought of going to see Mrs. Gailbraith, the twins' mother, but knew that she had been seasick since the boat left England. Elspeth didn't think the doctor would listen to her, with so many people ill, but she would have to try.

She made Robbie as comfortable as she could, then walked slowly through the hold, wondering whom she could ask for help. Perhaps it was a trick of the shadows, perhaps it was fear of the storm, but every face seemed to stare back at her with forbidding looks of bitterness or anger. Near the doorway, she saw Mrs. Beattie, the woman who had shared their compartment on the train. She was sitting on a wooden crate beside her bunk, looking straight ahead, and there was certainly nothing about her hard, carved features that made her face any less intimidating than the others. But at least she was familiar.

"Please, ma'am," said Elspeth, pausing beside her. "My wee brother's awful sick and I need help."

The woman turned slowly and looked at Elspeth, her expression not changing at all.

"Where do you think I'd find the doctor, ma'am?" Elspeth asked.

"Bring the lad here," Mrs. Beattie said in a flat voice. "There's more air here near the door."

"I don't know if I can carry him, ma'am," said Elspeth, fighting back tears. "He's awful bad."

"Jim!" said the woman, raising her voice. "Give the girl a hand to fetch her brother here. He's been sick."

Jim Beattie dragged himself slowly from the bunk beside them and followed Elspeth back to their corner. He waited while Elspeth helped Robbie out. She hoped Robbie wouldn't shout and struggle, thinking that one of *them* had got him, but he lay passive in Jim Beattie's arms.

"Have you given him anything to drink?" Mrs. Beattie asked when she saw him.

"It just makes him sick," said Elspeth.

Mrs. Beattie held a cup of water to Robbie's lips. He would have gulped it down, but she allowed him only a sip and then made him rest.

"You can leave him here for now," Mrs. Beattie said. "You should get a bit of air, or maybe have a sleep yourself. You look worn out."

Reluctantly, Elspeth left Robbie with Mrs. Beattie and climbed the stair to the deserted deck. She squeezed between the lifeboat and the rail, pulling the piece of loose canvas around her to cut off some of the wind. It was lonely here without Robbie. That Mrs. Beattie was a strange woman—the way she never asked about them being on their own.

Late in the afternoon the wind dropped. When Elspeth went back to the hold, she found that the lamps were lit again. People's faces looked softer now, kinder.

"How's Robbie?" she asked Mrs. Beattie.

"Much better," the woman answered. "He's had a cup of tea and a bite of bread and held it down. He's sleeping quite soundly now, so you'd best leave him here for tonight."

Elspeth wished that Mrs. Beattie would ask her to stay too, but she was staring straight ahead again, as if she had forgotten about Elspeth. Sadly Elspeth returned to their corner, which seemed very empty without Robbie. She smoothed out her blankets and lay down. Surely she was tired enough to sleep. Someone began to play the melody of the hymn "Lead Kindly Light." Elspeth listened to the words as people nearby joined in the singing. *The night is dark, and I am far from home: lead Thou me on.* "Please let Robbie be all right," she prayed over and over, until she finally fell asleep.

Elspeth awakened with a start. From the sounds around her she could tell that it was morning. For a moment she was alarmed to find that Robbie wasn't there, until she remembered that he was with Mrs. Beattie. She wriggled out of their corner and scampered down the hold in her eagerness to see him.

He was sitting on the edge of Mrs. Beattie's bunk, his face clean and his hair neatly brushed. His face lit up when he saw Elspeth.

"Where's Pig-Bear?" he asked. "Can we go outside?"

"You can take him up on the deck for a bit," Mrs. Beattie said. "The air is fresher there, but keep him out of the wind. He mustn't get cold, and don't let him run about."

"Thank you very much, ma'am," Elspeth said earnestly. "Robbie, say thank you."

Robbie leaned against Elspeth, twirling his hair with his forefinger, and smiled shyly at Mrs. Beattie.

But she had settled herself on the crate and was staring off into the distance. After a few uncertain moments, Elspeth and Robbie went to fetch Pig-Bear and then climbed the stairs to the deck.

Rebecca and Rachel were waiting beside the lifeboats. "Mama's awfully sick, so Papa sent us out," Rachel said. "Can we play Shadow Bairns?"

Elspeth shook her head. "Robbie's been sick too, and he mustn't run about. But I'll tell you more about Manitoba—the place we're going to."

With the ship cutting through the choppy sea, and Robbie better, Elspeth felt in touch with the future again. She began to describe the winding streets of Manitoba, the brick houses, the flower gardens.

She was unaware that Matthew had joined them and was also listening until he interrupted. "You've got it all wrong! Manitoba isn't a town. It's a country."

"Canada's the country," argued Elspeth. "Manitoba's just a place there. It's where my Aunt Maud and Uncle Donald live."

"Manitoba's part of Canada, all right. But it's as big as a country," Matthew insisted. "It's ten times bigger than Scotland."

"Ten times bigger than Scotland!" echoed Elspeth. "Then how would you find someone there?"

"I don't see that you could," answered Matthew. "Not if all you knew was that they lived in Manitoba."

Elspeth stared at Matthew, the color draining from her cheeks.

"All this about Shadow Bairns—and going to find your aunt and uncle. . . . You mean it's all true?" he asked slowly.

Elspeth nodded.

"You're just by yourselves? Alone?"

Elspeth nodded again.

"I thought your ma was seasick, like mine. I'm always being told to keep these two out of the way."

"We don't have any ma or pa to tell us what to do," said Elspeth in a low voice. "This woman came, and she was going to put Robbie in an orphanage and get me a job as a maid, but I'd promised Ma to look after Rob—so we ran away."

"But how did you get here by yourselves? Are you stowaways?" asked Matthew, amazed.

"Oh, no!" said Elspeth. "Papa had bought the boat tickets before—before—"

"How did you get to Liverpool?"

"That wasn't hard. I used to take Robbie to the station all the time to watch the trains. There's a board that tells where the trains are going. We used to pretend—"

"But it's not just getting the right train. . . ." Matthew's voice trailed off as he thought back over the way his ma and pa had discussed and argued about what they should take and what they should leave behind, what they'd need on the boat, and what they'd need once they got to Saskatoon. They had worried about what day to travel and where to stay in Liverpool. He couldn't possibly have managed without his family, and he was older than Elspeth.

Imagine being on his own with just Rachel or Rebecca. . . .

"So your aunt and uncle don't know you're coming?"

"No," Elspeth admitted. "There wasn't time to write, and anyway, I don't know their address."

"When did they go to Manitoba? Will they remember you?"

"They went six years ago, before Robbie was born, so they don't know about him. Before they went we had a big party at the croft—a *ceilidh*, we called it. Uncle Donald played the pipes. I remember my cousins dancing—Mary and Charlie and wee Donald. Wild, they were!"

"You might have more cousins by now—after six years," Matthew pointed out.

And they might not want her and Robbie. At that moment, Elspeth faced the awful truth that the Aunt Maud and Uncle Donald in the stories she told Rob were no more like the real people than her picture of Manitoba was like the real place. The night of the *ceilidh* was suddenly vivid in her mind. The cottage had been filled with the exciting sound of Uncle Donald's pipes; but she had stood by Mama, afraid to join in the dancing. Aunt Maud had called her a plain wee thing and had said she liked to see more spirit in a child. "She's not used to so many people," Mama had said, making excuses for her, but Aunt Maud had just tossed her black curls and gone off dancing with Papa, leaving Mama and Elspeth by themselves, watching. Maybe Aunt Maud wouldn't like her any better now than she did then. And she wasn't sure that she would like Aunt Maud. It was Mama and Papa she really wanted, and Aunt Maud wasn't a bit like Mama. Even Uncle Donald wasn't like Papa, although they were brothers.

"Don't just sit there," Rachel said, interrupting her thoughts. "Tell us more of the story."

"Matthew can tell it," said Elspeth. "He knows more about this place Manitoba than I do."

"But what are you going to do?" Matthew asked, not paying any attention to Rachel.

"I'll ask Mr. Barr to help me. He'll know how to find Uncle Donald," Elspeth answered, although she was no longer sure that this was what she wanted.

"Isaac Barr!" Matthew shouted. "Talking to *him* won't help. Pa says he's just out for himself. He doesn't trust him, and lots of others on this ship don't either."

"But he's a minister," protested Elspeth. "He's got to help people."

"Being a minister doesn't make any difference. Not with him."

"But he promised to find farms for people, and to help them."

"And he promised us a decent boat to sail in," scoffed Matthew.

"What's wrong with this one?" Elspeth asked defiantly.

"It's an old cattle ship," said Matthew. "Where the whitewash is flaking off the walls you can see manure. And it was meant to hold about eight hundred people and he has crammed in more than two thousand. If that's how it is now, do you think it will be any better in Canada?"

"I don't want to listen to you," said Elspeth. "I've talked to him and he feels—responsible for us."

"And well he should—he's got our money."

Suddenly Elspeth felt defeated. "What am I going to do?" she asked.

Matthew shrugged. "Maybe someone will help you when we get there." Then he added hopefully, "After all, the government must keep records of all the land they give away—so they don't give it away twice. Someone must know where your aunt and uncle settled."

"But suppose they don't want us? Suppose they haven't room?"

"You should have thought of that sooner. It's a bit late now."

"Maybe I can get work."

"You don't look old enough," said Matthew. "Now if it was me, I could get a job on a farm. But there's not going to be much call for girls building houses or breaking in new land."

"You're horrible! I hate you!" Elspeth shouted. All her anger and frustration were suddenly centered on Matthew. It was all right for him to be so sure of himself. He was fourteen years old, big for his age, and a boy besides. But it wasn't his problem they were talking about.

Matthew was surprised by Elspeth's sudden burst of temper, and when she grabbed Robbie, saying it was time to go inside, he didn't follow.

That was the end of playing Shadow Bairns for Elspeth. She had no heart for it now. Matthew, the twins, and Robbie still played, and other children were drawn into the game. It reached a great climax the day before the ship docked at St. John. The weather had changed, and they were shrouded by fog so thick that their whole world was no bigger than the overcrowded ship. All day long the foghorn sounded its melancholy note, but for Shadow Bairns it was perfect weather. Dozens of children glided about the deck like gray phantoms, dodging, hiding, and pouncing on one another in a game that lasted all day long.

But for Elspeth there was only worry. She had embarked on a journey with no destination beyond the fog.

# 6

## "Drawbacks"

### APRIL 10–17

ON GOOD FRIDAY THE SUN BROKE THROUGH THE FOG, and the passengers on the *Lake Manitoba* caught their first glimpse of the New Land. Even Elspeth, standing at the rail with Robbie, shared the feeling of hope and excitement. But enthusiasm changed to impatience when people learned that there were no trains waiting at St. John to meet the boat. Impatience was fanned to anger when rumors spread that Isaac Barr had bought up all the flour on the boat and had ordered it to be made into loaves, which he was selling for twice as much as the bakers charged in St. John. But people bought the bread, for it would be needed on the long train journey to Saskatoon.

Elspeth and Robbie went down to the dining room, hoping to get a meal. They found it packed with people, but no sign of food.

"Don't we get any dinner?" Elspeth asked a steward. "What's everyone doing?"

"The bankers have come aboard from St. John with Canadian money, so everyone's changing their pound notes into dollars."

"Changing their pound notes," Elspeth repeated, puzzled.

"Aye. You need dollars for spending in Canada," explained the steward.

Elspeth realized that she was going to need some of these dollars, but would the bankers change money for a girl? Or would they ask a lot of questions about where the money came from? At last she said to Robbie, "Do you think you could find Matthew and bring him here?"

Robbie nodded eagerly and scampered away. Elspeth, meantime, went down to the hold. She hurriedly took two bundles of pound notes from the bodice of her skirt. She wasn't going to part with all her pounds until she was sure that these strange Canadian dollars were real money.

Matthew and Robbie were waiting outside the dining room when she came back. She didn't like asking a favor of Matthew, but when she explained, he only said, "So you do have money! I'd been wondering about that." He pushed his way eagerly into the crowd.

After some time, he returned, disheveled but triumphant. "I got it!" he told Elspeth. "But let's get away from here. There's going to be trouble. The bankers are out of dollars and can't get more until after Easter. Everyone's blaming Barr."

Elspeth wanted to point out that it wasn't Isaac Barr's fault that the bankers hadn't brought enough money with them, but decided that now wasn't the time for another argument with Matthew. Instead, she thanked him and went down to the hold to hide her money.

Two days later, on Easter Sunday, the air was filled, not with the sound of hymns, but with the creak of cranes, the crash of shunting engines, and the raised voices of the crowd. Trains were at last waiting, but the dock was so congested with baggage that there wasn't room for the passengers to disembark until the cranes were finally halted.

The Canadian officials on shore, waiting to check papers and tickets, shook their heads in disbelief at the accumulating piles of boxes, trunks, sofas, and even pianos. Hadn't anyone told these people of the difficulty and hardship of travel in the west? And where was this Isaac Barr, who was supposed to be in charge?

Elspeth, dragging their traveling bag and clutching Robbie by the hand, was near the front of the crowd surging down the gangplank. She looked around, hoping to see the twins or Matthew. She had the papers and tickets from Papa's box ready. There was no reason why they shouldn't let her into Canada, she told herself. She straightened her shoulders, wishing she looked older.

Suddenly they were on firm ground. Robbie, who had become so sure-footed on the lurching deck, stumbled and fell flat in a puddle formed by recently melted snow, dropping Pig-Bear. Elspeth rescued Pig-Bear, wiped Robbie off as best she could, and begged him to be a brave boy. Men pushed past, ignoring them in their eagerness to get through

Customs and onto the trains. When Robbie's cries had quieted to intermittent sniffs, Elspeth joined the crowd again.

"Who's next?" a stern-looking official demanded, looking over Elspeth's head.

"Me, sir!" Elspeth answered timidly.

"Where's your pa?" the man asked impatiently. "Who's with these children?"

No one came forward to claim them, but the next man in line thrust his papers under the official's nose.

"Stand there and watch for your ma and pa," the man told Elspeth, gesturing toward the end of the table.

Elspeth, holding Robbie firmly, moved off to the side. The official picked up the next man's papers. Confronted by some new problem, he began to question him. Then, like Shadow Bairns again, Elspeth and Robbie merged with the crowd of people heading through the station entrance.

The station was disappointingly unlike the one in Glasgow. There was no departure board to tell Elspeth how to get to Manitoba or anywhere else. The train, standing beside the platform with its doors gaping open, looked very big and foreign. Its great wedge-shaped cowcatcher in front, the clanging bell on top, and carriages so high above the platform that people had to climb steps to reach the doors, looked strange to Elspeth and Robbie.

Farther down the platform Elspeth saw a uniformed official coming toward them. "Come on,

Robbie! This way!" She pulled Robbie across the platform and up the steps to the train, heaving their bag and bundle of blankets on ahead of them.

Inside, the train wasn't divided into compartments the way the one in Glasgow had been, nor were the seats covered with red velvet. Instead they were in a long coach with seats made of slatted wood.

"We'll sit here," Elspeth said, pushing Robbie onto a seat. He sat quietly, sucking on Pig-Bear's ear, watching wide-eyed as the passengers filed into the train. Elspeth wished they could see some of the children they knew from the boat, but there were only men, most of them quite young.

"Is this the right train? Should we be here?" Robbie asked, giving voice to Elspeth's own doubts.

"Of course it's the right train," Elspeth answered sharply. "I didn't see any other."

Someone outside shouted to a few late arrivals who were running toward their coach, dragging bags and bundles. Doors banged shut down the length of the train, a bell clanged, and the engine got up steam.

After the train started, Robbie sat quietly looking out the window, but then he began to experiment with the venetian blind. It came rattling down, frightening both Elspeth and himself.

"Do sit still, and let things be," Elspeth said crossly. She could see that it was going to be hard to keep Robbie amused on the train after the freedom he had had on the boat. She wished again that there were other children.

"Can we walk about?" Robbie asked.

"Maybe later," Elspeth promised. "But sit still for now." She didn't want to leave her seat and meet the curious gaze of all these men.

"I have been sitting still—for a long time," Robbie complained.

The argument was cut short by the appearance of the train conductor. Elspeth's heart pounded at the sight of a uniform—people in uniforms always seemed like *them*. She turned away and stared hard out the window.

"What are *you* doing here?" the conductor asked, stopping beside them. "I was told that there were just single men on this train. People with children were to travel together on the third train. So what in the name of heaven are two bairns doing here?" He took off his cap and ran his fingers through his graying hair.

He spoke in a soft Highland voice, just like their father's. So much like his that Robbie looked up at the man, held out his arms, and wailed, "I want Papa! I want Papa!"

"Don't tell me you children got on the wrong train.

Elspeth nodded, not knowing what else to say. After all, it was true. They were on the wrong train, and they were by themselves.

"I can't turn the train back, you know. What am I going to do with you?"

"I want Papa!" Robbie wailed again.

"And he'll be wanting you," said the man. "How

did you manage to get on this train by yourselves? Though from what I saw of that mess on the dock it will be a wonder if there are only *two* lost bairns. But to get on the train alone! Such a bother your mama and papa will be in. Did you never think of that?"

Elspeth, who had managed to control her tears for so long, began to sob. It wasn't the man's scolding. It was the way he made Mama and Papa seem real again—as if there was someone who cared.

"Crying will help nothing," he said severely. "I could put you off in Montreal to wait for their train, but you still might miss them, and I wouldn't feel right leaving you there alone."

In his preoccupation, he ran his fingers through his hair again, then crammed on his cap so that his hair stuck out in unruly tufts.

"Maybe it would be better to have you bide here where I can keep an eye on you. I'll send a telegram to St. John telling your parents that you're on this train, and then I'll put you in the care of someone when we get to Saskatoon till your papa gets there. Yes, that would be the best way," he said, nodding to himself. "I'll need your names so that I can send the telegram."

"Elspeth and Robert MacDonald," Elspeth whispered.

"And your mama and papa?"

Elspeth hesitated and then said, "Margaret and Duncan MacDonald."

Muttering to himself, the conductor left them and

continued on his way down the train. Robbie rose from his seat, as if to follow him, but Elspeth pulled him back.

"He's going to find Mama and Papa, isn't he?" Robbie asked in a breathless voice.

"No, he's not," Elspeth answered harshly.

"But he said . . . you said . . ." Robbie's voice trailed off hesitantly.

"Never mind what I said!" Elspeth leaned her forehead against the cold glass of the window, wishing now that she had told the man the truth. He seemed nice, not busy and disinterested like the social worker. But it was so hard to tell about people.

A few minutes later, the conductor returned with two mugs of soup, which he handed to Rob and Elspeth. "You can't buy meals on this train," he said. "There's stoves at the end of each coach, and water, but that's not much use if you haven't brought your own food or anything to cook it in. You might get something at·the stations, but I don't suppose you have money."

"I have a little," Elspeth admitted cautiously.

But the conductor saw to it that they had something to eat whenever a mealtime came around. He became very fond of Robbie. He took him down the train to see the engine driver, and didn't seem to mind that Robbie was soon spending most of the day in his company.

Elspeth knew that she would have had a hard time keeping Robbie entertained on so long a train ride, but she missed having him to talk to. She stared out the window at the ever-changing yet never-changing scene. It was a cold land, still in the grip of winter. An empty land—rugged, vast, and lonely. After Montreal, the few stations where they stopped had an air of impermanence, with wooden platforms and rough buildings. The towns were not yet part of the total landscape the way they were in Scotland. Sometimes she saw abandoned clearings and gaunt, burned trees, which must have spelled the end of some pioneer's dreams.

From the talk going on around her, Elspeth found out that after the train reached Saskatoon, they still had to travel two hundred miles north to reach the Barr colony. There was no railroad up there, not even a proper road. Looking at the country they were passing through gave her an idea of how hard this might be. Yet people were talking about buying plows and cattle and supplies in Saskatoon. Someone said that Barr was going to organize a wagon train, but most of the men seemed to doubt that he would. Anyway, they didn't intend to wait around to see. They planned to go north on their own.

On the fourth day, the train crossed the Province of Manitoba. Robbie was too busy listening to songs and watching noisy card games to be disappointed that it wasn't at all like the place Elspeth had described on the boat. But all day Elspeth sat staring out the window, wondering what she and Robbie should do.

Some of the men were going to leave the train in Winnipeg, saying they'd sooner be on their own than depend on Barr. "It's better to get land in an area that's already settled," one of them argued. "That way you can learn from those who have been here awhile."

Elspeth wondered if she and Robbie should get out in Winnipeg, too, and begin their search for Uncle Donald. There was no sense in going all the way to Saskatoon only to have to come back. But she didn't know how to escape from the kindly watchfulness of the train conductor. He always made sure they were aboard after each stop. There was no way to tell him now about Uncle Donald and Aunt Maud, after letting him think that they had parents worrying about them in St. John. Besides, how would she set about looking for Uncle Donald in a place where there was so much land and so few people? And there was the gnawing thought that she wouldn't like Aunt Maud. Even worse—that Aunt Maud and Uncle Donald might not want them.

Elspeth stared out at the flat, treeless land, knowing that there was still another reason why she didn't want to leave the train. In spite of what everybody said, she believed in Mr. Barr. After all, *she* had spoken to him, and he had said that she was the sort of person the colony needed—young and willing to learn. And Papa had been so excited about being part of this venture, about owning land that would someday belong to his children and their children. As long as she stayed with the Barr colonists there seemed to be a thread linking her to Papa's dreams, a thread that would be broken if she turned to Uncle Donald and asked for charity.

What was it that Isaac Barr had said in his pamphlet? *There are difficulties and drawbacks to be encountered; but for the brave man obstacles are something to be overcome.* There were plenty of obstacles in her path, but there must be a way around them. She would find Mr. Barr and explain to him why they had come by themselves. Maybe he would let them stay with him until they were old enough to farm on their own. As a minister he would need a maid to keep the place clean and answer the door. She would work really hard, and Robbie would be no trouble at all.

Isaac Barr wasn't on their train, so Elspeth decided that when they arrived in Saskatoon, she and Robbie would find somewhere to stay until she had a chance to speak to him. She had plenty of money. There must be hotels because others spoke of spending a few days in Saskatoon getting their outfits together for the journey north. She tried not to think about what she would do if Mr. Barr wouldn't help her.

On their last day on the train everyone seemed as bored as Elspeth was and as restless as Robbie. Even the card players had lost interest in their game. There was only one man who wanted to continue. He was Geoffrey Whitcomb, a thin man with lank hair that flopped down over his forehead. Elspeth gathered that he had lost a lot of money gambling, because his younger brother was angry, saying that the money had been for both of them.

"Don't worry so much, Arthur! I'll win it back," Geoffrey assured him. "And if not, Father can send us more. He said he would if we found things tight out here."

"He said no such thing, Geoffrey!"

"Well, he should have," said Geoffrey sullenly. "It's hardly fair that Edgar inherits Rainwater Manor while we get shipped off to this awful place. There should be a law protecting younger sons."

"You could have stayed at Cambridge," Arthur pointed out.

"You know I couldn't! They expelled me!" Geoffrey answered. However, the thought of Cambridge University seemed to cheer him up. "Too bad you never got to go there, Arthur," he said.

"You know I didn't want to go. I wanted to see Canada."

"And now you're seeing it!" answered Geoffrey. "Not exactly my idea of the Promised Land!"

The rhythm of the train began to change as it approached a station and slowed down.

"Don't tell me this is Saskatoon that we've been hearing so much about!" Geoffrey said in tones of despair.

Elspeth stared out the window. Even she had expected more. Saskatoon was scarcely more than a village, hemmed in by a river and the prairie. A few wooden houses and small stores were scattered on the east side of the railway track. The only building of any size was the Government Immigration Building. The station was a small shack, not nearly big enough to accommodate all the passengers. When the train came to a stop, everyone scrambled down onto the bare prairie. Someone helped Elspeth with her bag and lifted Robbie down beside her.

"What's going to happen now?" Robbie asked.

Elspeth had no answer.

# 7

## "Stay at home— don't come to Canada"

### APRIL 17

"THEY'VE HAD NO WORD AT THE RAILWAY STATION about your parents," the conductor said to Elspeth in a worried voice. "Let me take your bag and we'll go and see the immigration people. Maybe they will know something."

The spring thaw had turned the unpaved streets to rivers of mud. The mud splashed Elspeth's woolen stockings and caked her shoes as she followed the kindly conductor to the Immigration Building. This place was dirtier and shabbier than Glasgow. It was hard to tell if half the buildings were going up or falling down. And the wind was so cold that Elspeth welcomed the thought of getting indoors, even if it meant confronting another official. She wasn't sure how much she should say—or what Robbie might say—but at least they'd tell her where the hotel was.

When they reached the building, the conductor ushered them inside, saying cheerfully to a red-faced man who was sitting behind a desk, "I've got two lost bairns here. They got on the wrong train back in

New Brunswick. Have you heard from their parents?"

"Lost children! Just what we need!" the man answered in an irritated voice. "Leave them here and I'll see if I can straighten things out."

"They're good bairns," the conductor said. "I'd be proud of them if they were mine."

"There's something I want to tell you before you go," Elspeth said timidly. Suddenly she was tired of deceiving everybody. The train conductor, with his soft voice like Papa's, would surely understand.

"No, no!" he said, waving her aside. "No need to say anything. You don't owe me thanks. I've enjoyed the journey with you bairns along. As I said before, your father and mother are lucky people. It is a fine pair of children they have!"

He pulled a small bag of barley sugar out of his pocket and handed it to Elspeth, ruffled Rob's hair, and was gone, swallowed up in a crowd of people coming into the building. Elspeth stood there, unable to finish what she had been about to say.

"I had something to tell him," she said wildly to the immigration officer. "We don't have anyone coming on another train. We're all alone—just by ourselves."

Until now, the man had been only mildly annoyed by their problem. Now he turned his full attention on Elspeth, staring at her with incredulous eyes.

"Say that again!" he thundered.

"We're all by ourselves. No one's coming on

another train. You see, our Mama and Papa are dead."

"This beats everything!" he said, throwing up his hands. "Isaac Moses Barr and his colony! Bringing all these people here without first making proper arrangements for food and accommodation. Two thousand people dumped on a town of four hundred inhabitants! And who's having to bail him out? The Canadian government—that's who! And now this! Orphans—walking in here and telling me they're on their own—that they came out with the colony. I tell you, we're setting up no orphanage here. If it's the only thing I get done today, I'm sending you back where you came from. This is one thing that Barr doesn't get away with."

Elspeth stared at the man, not able to understand why he was so angry, or even who he was so angry with. But one thing she did know—in finally telling someone the truth she had made a big mistake. This man was one of *them*.

He took Elspeth and Robbie into a small, cluttered back room with high windows, and told them to sit down on the only two chairs. The table was overflowing with papers and dirty mugs and ash trays that needed emptying. Another man joined them, a dark, swarthy man with a big moustache. The two men towered over the children, both asking questions.

"Could I stay here till I can talk to Mr. Barr, sir?" Elspeth asked timidly. "You see, on the boat—"

The mention of Mr. Barr seemed to make the immigration officer angrier.

Elspeth explained that they had had tickets, and had as much right to be on the boat as anyone else. Maybe if they helped her find Uncle Donald in Manitoba. . . . No one listened to her. But for some reason, they did listen when Robbie suddenly spoke up and said that they had been Shadow Bairns on the boat.

"What's this about Shadow Bairns?" the dark man asked.

"We played all over the boat," said Robbie, brightening up at the memory of the fun they had had. "We hid everywhere."

"Shadow Bairns are quiet," Elspeth whispered savagely.

"How many of you were there?"

"Lots," said Robbie.

"Just us two," said Elspeth at the same time.

"They've shipped us a whole orphanage, that's what they've done!" said the bald man, sweat glistening on his forehead. "Children hiding all over the ship. It's some kind of invasion."

He glared at Elspeth and Robbie as if they were a species of rodent that was about to overrun Canada. They shrank back in their chairs.

"An invasion! Now that's a bit far-fetched," said the other man. "Though I still don't see how these two came all this way on their own. Why weren't they stopped at St. John?"

"They ship us all these people they don't have jobs for in the Old Country," said the first man, warming to his idea. "Why not carry it one step farther and send us their unwanted children? I tell you, they've sent us a shipload of orphans."

"That's not true!" said Elspeth, suddenly feeling more angry than frightened. "We came on our own. We had tickets like everybody else. Anyway, I'm nearly fourteen. I'm too old for an orphanage. I want to get a job as a maid."

But Elspeth's outburst was ignored. She fought back tears of frustration, realizing that she couldn't convince them she was old enough to look after herself and Robbie, and it wouldn't help if she began to cry.

"I won't believe there are more until I see them," said the man with the moustache.

"I'm going to have the next train stopped and searched before it gets here. I don't *want* to see more of them. You heard the lad say there were lots of them. I'll send a telegram now." He went over to the desk, pushing aside papers in his search for a pencil.

"And be the laughingstock of the department, George! Keep it in perspective. We have two lost children. Why would they be here on their own if they're part of a bigger group?"

"They could have been sent ahead to find out about the place." His voice trailed off as he looked at the children again. They weren't the type you'd choose for spies—the girl with her ill-fitting clothes and thin, white face, the boy with untied boots, a runny nose, jacket buttoned wrong, and hanging onto a battered toy. The man took a red hankerchief from his pocket and mopped his brow. His imagination was getting out of control, but this whole scheme of Barr's was so overblown that he had reached the stage when no idea was too bizarre.

"It's all the fault of the immigration people in St. John," he said angrily, looking for someone else to blame. "They're responsible and they can decide what to do with them. They should never have let children into the country without someone to sign for them. We'll put them on the eastbound train tomorrow, and I'll telegraph the people at St. John to expect them. There's no place for them here."

"And what do we do with them till tomorrow?" the dark man asked.

"They can sleep in one of the tents across the tracks."

"Will they be warm enough?"

"They've got blankets, haven't they?" the bald man asked, turning his back on them and leaving the room.

The other man picked up the suitcase, and Elspeth and Robbie followed him timidly. He stopped at the door and asked if they had eaten supper. When Elspeth shook her head, he took them to a crowded store where he bought cold sausage, bread, and milk. Now that he was on his own Elspeth found him less alarming, and tried once more to make him see that it would be easier for everyone if he would help her find Uncle Donald, or at least let them wait and talk to Mr. Barr. No one wanted them in St. John, or even back in Scotland.

"Rules are rules," the man answered firmly. "This is a new country, and there's no place for you here."

On the other side of the railway tracks, tents were sprouting up like pointed mushrooms on the edge of the prairie. Robbie kept stumbling and tripping over guy ropes as the man led them through the maze of tents.

"I'll put you in here," he said, opening the flap of a big army tent. "This one has a floor in it, which makes it a bit warmer than sleeping on the ground. With the ice only just gone out of the river it's still cold at nights."

The tent was big and bare and smelled of wet canvas.

"There'll be seven or eight families in here tomorrow night," the man told Elspeth. "It won't seem so empty then!"

"The families will be here tomorrow?" Elspeth asked.

"Tomorrow or the next day. Most will stay in the tents for a week or two, getting ready for the trip north, and we've put up more tents along the route. By rights, Isaac Barr should have been making all these arrangements."

"How long do you think Mr. Barr will stay here?"

"My guess is that he'll go right up to Battleford. That's the only place between here and the colony, and it would make sense for him to set up his headquarters there. Not that this enterprise runs on good sense! But I shouldn't be here talking—I've work to do."

When the man left, Robbie began to cry. "I'm cold," he whimpered. "I don't like it here."

Robbie's tear-stained face looked pinched and sallow. Elspeth hoped that it was just the effect of the greenish light filtering through the canvas and not that he was going to be sick again. She unrolled the blankets and began to make up their bed.

"Do we have to go on the train again? I'm tired of the train," Robbie said. "Where's Uncle Donald's house?"

Elspeth folded a blanket in half, smoothing out the wrinkles. She couldn't bear the thought of the train either. It would be empty this time, so Rob would be more bored than ever. She thought fleetingly that maybe they could get out in Winnipeg and look for Uncle Donald, but who would help her find him? Not the immigration people! A better plan might be to hide in Saskatoon—at least until the next train came. Maybe Matthew and the twins could help her, and maybe she would see Mr. Barr.

"Let's take a look around before it gets dark, Robbie," Elspeth said, taking him by the hand. She led him between the tents back to the railway track where they stood unnoticed on the fringe of the activity. Some men were still claiming luggage from the station, while others were asking where to get wagons and carts and supplies. A few lucky ones, with enough ready cash, had already bought wagons and horses and were loading up their belongings.

Elspeth wondered if she and Rob could stow away among the bundles, but watching how boxes and supplies were jammed into the carts, she gave up that idea.

Maybe, if she could find a job in one of the stores, the immigration man would let them stay. They walked back to the main street, but the storekeeper was so gruff and busy that Elspeth didn't have the courage to speak to him. Disconsolately, she and Robbie trailed their way back to the tent city. Beyond the tents they could see the road that led north across the endless prairie. It was not really a road at all—just two wheel marks that met at a point in the distance. Not a trail for Shadow Bairns. There was no place to hide.

The big empty tent now seemed as lonely as the vast prairie. Robbie's teeth were chattering, so Elspeth wrapped him in a blanket before dividing out the food for their supper. Outside, Elspeth could hear voices. As she listened, she realized that it was the Whitcomb brothers who had been on the train. They were still arguing about money.

"That was our last seventy-five dollars, Geoffrey! Even if he holds the pony and cart for us for a day, there's no way we can get more money by then."

"I can pick up fifty dollars at a card game tonight."

"No one's interested in cards tonight," Arthur answered. "They're all in too much of a hurry to head north. I'm tired of your surefire ways of making money. Look where it's landed us now!"

Elspeth whispered, "You stay here, Robbie. I'm going to ask them something."

She gave Robbie a piece of the conductor's barley sugar to comfort him and then slipped outside the tent. She walked right up to the two young men, but they continued to talk, ignoring her.

"I'll pay you if you'll give me and my brother a ride to Battleford," she said nervously.

"What did you say?" Geoffrey asked, finally noticing her.

"We want to get to Battleford. I'll give you fifty dollars if you'll take me and my brother."

"It's the children from the train," Arthur said. "What are you doing on your own, anyway? And why the hurry to get to Battleford?"

"We're going to stay with our uncle and aunt because our parents died," Elspeth said. She thought of telling the whole story, but they would only say that there was no place for them in Canada, and by now she knew that mentioning Mr. Barr's name never helped either.

"Your uncle and aunt are in Battleford?" Geoffrey asked suspiciously.

"My uncle didn't get down here to meet us, like he hoped to, so we were going to ride up with—with the Galbraiths, who were our friends on the boat, but this man in the Immigration Building says we have to go back to St. John because no one signed papers for us. That's not fair because we paid for our tickets to come here," Elspeth finished breathlessly.

Elspeth wasn't sure that her story made sense, but Geoffrey was more interested in her troubles with the immigration officer than in her uncle. "Was he a red-faced fellow with shoulders like a bull?" he asked. "Is he the one who's sending you back?"

Elspeth nodded.

"He's the one who won't let you file for a claim because you're six weeks short of eighteen, Arthur!" Turning back to Elspeth, Geoffrey added. "He says Arthur can't file until his birthday, and by that time there won't be adjoining sections on decent land."

"If you'll take us, I'll pay you fifty dollars," Elspeth repeated.

"Let's take them, Arthur," Geoffrey said. "We'll spite old Bullface. He'd never suspect us, and with the fifty dollars we could pay for the pony and cart."

"But suppose this uncle isn't waiting in Battleford," said Arthur, still the more cautious of the two.

"If he's not there, I have to stay in the hotel till he comes," Elspeth said quickly. "I have enough money for that."

"And what about food?" Arthur asked. "We've hardly enough for ourselves."

"Let's see this money," said Geoffrey. "You don't look like you have fifty dollars."

Elspeth ducked back inside the tent. It was almost too dark to see. With trembling fingers, she unpicked the stitches that held the money hidden in the bodice of her skirt. She gave Robbie another piece of barley sugar and went back outside.

Geoffrey and Arthur were arguing again, their

voices now pitched too low for her to hear. She counted the money into Geoffrey's hand. "Fifty-five dollars. The extra is to pay for our food."

"Five dollars!" Geoffrey snorted. "It will take us more than five days to get there, and do you know what they're asking for a loaf of bread in this place?"

Five days! Elspeth hadn't thought about Battleford being so far away, but she concealed her surprise. "We don't eat much," she said. "Get some oatmeal. I can make porridge."

"Maybe we'll be glad to have a cook along!" Geoffrey said with a laugh.

"We'll have to get away early," Elspeth said.

"We'll be early," Geoffrey assured her. "If we're smuggling you out of Saskatoon, then we don't want to get caught any more than you do."

They walked away, leaving Elspeth empty-handed. When they disappeared behind the next tent, Elspeth wondered if she would see them again. Maybe she and Robbie would be on the train tomorrow, fifty-five dollars poorer, while the Whitcomb brothers headed north, pleased to have come by the money they needed so easily.

She went back into the tent where she shared out the sausage, bread, and milk. It was the best supper they had had for days, and there was some left over for breakfast. Elspeth felt cheered as she lay down on the floor to sleep, but the floor soon felt hard and cold. The night was full of unexpected noises—the bark of a dog, the moaning wind, the constant slapping of a piece of loose canvas. Robbie fell asleep, snuffling slightly, but Elspeth lay awake. A fragment of a hymn they sang on the boat ran through her mind. *I do not ask to see the distant scene—one step enough for me.* She'd worry about what to do in Battleford when she got there.

# 8

# "On the surface of the soil"

## APRIL 18–19

ELSPETH WAS AWAKENED BY A SOUND OUTSIDE THE tent. Please, don't let it be the immigration man, she thought, as she slipped out of her blankets and peered anxiously through the tent opening. It was still dark, but she could make out two shadowy figures. Beside them stood a pony and a cart piled high with their belongings. The Whitcomb brothers had not betrayed her.

"We got it," whispered Arthur. "This is Sea Gull." The pony tossed its head as if greeting her. "I hope you don't have much luggage. We should get it loaded up quickly."

Elspeth ducked back into the tent and came out dragging the traveling bag and blankets. Robbie, hardly awake, clung to her skirt crying.

"Hush up, Robbie! You're going for a ride on the pony," Elspeth said.

"Oh no, he's not!" said Geoffrey. "We can't take him with us!"

"Why not? You said you'd take me and my brother," Elspeth said sharply.

"You didn't say he was just a baby!"

"I thought you'd seen him on the train," said Elspeth. "Do hush, Robbie!"

"He didn't seem so little then."

"You should be glad he's little with all that stuff you've got and only a small pony to pull it. He won't take up much room."

Geoffrey couldn't dispute this. "You'll have to make him be quiet," he said, and that was all.

Elspeth pulled the bag of barley sugar out of her pocket, and Robbie immediately stopped crying. With each passing minute the darkness was ebbing, and the tents now stood out clearly around them. It was light enough that anyone watching could see them leave.

As if reading Elspeth's thoughts, Geoffrey swung Robbie up onto the cart and sat him in a galvanized iron bathtub, saying, "We'll put the lad in here. He looks like he needs a bath anyway. You get up beside him, and I'll throw a blanket over both of you. When we're away from the town, you can take the blanket off."

Relieved that Geoffrey was no longer raising objections, Elspeth climbed up and pulled the blanket over her. Her heart pounding, she listened to the protesting creaks and groans of the cart as they passed between the tents, heading for the trail that led out across the prairie. Other people were awake now, and the smells of coffee and frying bacon made Elspeth hungry. She was digging around in a corner of their bag, trying to find where she had put the remains of last night's supper, when the cart jolted to a stop, nearly jerking her off the back. Robbie gave a squeak of protest.

"You lads are early on the trail," boomed a loud voice.

The immigration man! Elspeth huddled under the blanket, closing her eyes as if that would make her less visible. Shadow Bairns are quiet, she said over and over again in her mind, willing Robbie not to talk and give them away.

"We wanted to get out ahead of the rush," Arthur said.

"You'd be smarter to wait for a few other wagons so as not to be alone on the trail. There are sloughs to cross."

"We're not afraid of being alone," answered Geoffrey. "We don't expect much company where we're going. We may as well get used to being on our own now."

"You won't get across Eagle Creek with that outfit without help," the man warned them.

"We'll face that when we come to it," Geoffrey answered impatiently.

Elspeth let out a long breath of relief when the cart lurched forward again. Arthur started to sing, slightly off key, covering a burst of coughing from Robbie.

"All right back there?" he asked, some time later. "You can come out and take a look."

Elspeth threw back the blanket and found that Robbie had already wriggled out. He was sitting up, looking around. She gave him a piece of bread and sausage, and he munched on it happily.

The sun was climbing up the blue sky—a wider sky than Elspeth had ever seen before—dotted with fleecy white clouds that were scraped flat across the bottom as if they had touched the prairie. The wind tugged at the dead, brown grass, newly exposed by melting snow, and rippled through tender green grass that was bursting out of the earth. The wind was everywhere, pushing them back, pulling them on. Elspeth shook out her braids, letting it tug at her light brown hair. She could taste the wind, smell the wind, and hear it tell of faraway places.

Behind them lay Saskatoon. The government building that had been so big and forbidding yesterday was now just the size of a toy. The bald man inside would be so small that he didn't matter anymore. She felt a sudden surge of confidence. She loved this spacious land.

"Can we get down too?" she asked Geoffrey, who was walking beside the cart.

"We won't wait if you fall behind," he warned her.

By now Elspeth had discovered that Geoffrey wasn't as unfriendly as his sharp tongue made him seem. She jumped down and helped Robbie out. After so many days of sitting on the hard, slatted seat in the stuffy train it was wonderful to feel the springy turf under their feet. They walked carefully, trying not to step on the first early crocuses, and watched gophers scurry into their holes. The prairie wasn't nearly as flat as it had looked from the window of the train. The track led over humps and into hollows. Far ahead, they could see a great stretch of dazzling green. When Robbie grew tired, Geoffrey lifted him onto Sea Gull's back, but Elspeth kept on walking until they came to the edge of the bright green. It was just grass, but lush because it was growing in standing water. Here and there were clumps of rushes, and several mallards exploded into the air, disturbed by their arrival.

Arthur pulled Sea Gull to a stop, gazing anxiously at the indistinct trail ahead. The marsh grass was broken and flattened by wagons that had gone before, but then the wheel marks were lost in patches of water, ruffled by the wind and shimmering in the sunlight.

"This must be one of these sloughs they talk about," he said. "Maybe we should go around it."

"Looks like others have gone through," Geoffrey said. "Let me handle the horse. Elspeth, get up in the cart and hang on to your brother for all you're worth."

When Elspeth and Robbie were firmly wedged in the back of the cart, Geoffrey raised the whip and brought it down on poor Sea Gull's sagging back. He flinched and then strained forward, but before they reached firm ground, the heavy alkali mud dragging against the wheels proved too much for Sea Gull. Geoffrey tried coaxing, and then the whip again, but finally had to admit defeat.

They started to unload the cart, carrying the boxes and bundles to the other side of the slough. The heavy mud sucked at their feet. It was slippery too, and their muscles soon ached from the effort of keeping their balance. At last the load was light enough so that Sea Gull could drag the cart through. Then began the weary job of repacking. Nothing fit quite as well as it had before. Geoffrey was determined to make up for lost time when they started out again, and they rattled and jolted over the rough ground, boxes and bundles sliding and shifting in the cart. Even so, progress was slow. By nightfall they hadn't reached the first of the tents that had been erected by government officials at points along the trail.

"We've got a tent of our own," Arthur said to Elspeth. "And we can rig a tarpaulin between the cart and the ground for you and the lad. But first, let's have supper."

Elspeth hummed quietly to herself as she stirred a pot of beans over the camp stove. By the time they started eating, the stars were beginning to show in the darkened sky to the east, while the afterglow of the sun stained the western sky red. "This is the best meal we've had since we left England," Arthur said, helping himself to more beans. Elspeth glowed with pleasure, even though she knew that the meal owed more to appetites sharpened by a long day in the fresh air than to her cooking.

"And this has been my best day," Robbie said with a happy sigh. "I hope Uncle Donald has a pony just like Sea Gull."

The next morning they had only covered a few

miles when one of the front wheels struck a rock and
the cart lurched to a stop.

"A hundred and twenty-five dollars and the wheel
breaks the first time it hits a stone," Geoffrey said,
kicking two broken spokes in disgust.

It was by no means the first stone, but Elspeth
didn't point that out. Instead, she offered Geoffrey a
piece of barley sugar. She still wasn't at ease with
him, but he did need cheering up, and she didn't
have to save the candy to keep Robbie quiet out here
on the prairie.

Arthur began to fashion two new spokes out of
boards from the oak lid of a packing case, cutting and
whittling with surprising skill and patience. One or
two wagons overtook them while they were stopped.
As each one drew up beside them, to offer advice or
just to give a friendly greeting, Elspeth worried that
it might be the immigration official, but Geoffrey
laughed at her.

"You're not that important!" he said. "Besides,
with four more trains due from St. John, and Isaac
Barr to deal with, they can't spare men to stalk
Shadow Bairns!"

Robbie had told Geoffrey and Arthur about
playing Shadow Bairns on the boat. He also talked
about what he was going to do at Uncle Donald's
house—about the calf he was going to have, and how
he would play with his cousins, Mary and Charlie
and Donald, and their dog, Jock. He told them that
the house was white and the door was blue. Elspeth
felt a cold chill as she listened to Robbie talk with

such certainty about their destination, but at least Arthur no longer had doubts about Uncle Donald's existence.

When the wheel was finally repaired, Geoffrey drove more cautiously. Late in the afternoon, they came to another slough and once again became mired. This time the slough was much bigger. They carried boxes back to the side they had started from until the cart was light enough for Sea Gull to drag it back to firm ground. After they had loaded up again, they wondered what they should do. The swamp seemed to stretch for miles to the east and the west. They were unable to go straight ahead, but were reluctant to branch out from the trail they had been following. The country was so vast and lonely, so unlike anything they were used to, that they needed the reassurance of the wheel marks telling them that people had traveled this way before.

Suddenly Robbie said, "I see more horses coming." They counted eight wagons forming a straggling train back down the trail.

The first wagon pulled up beside them. The driver, a big burly man, leaned out and said, "William Reed's the name. How deep is this one?"

"About six inches of water, but heavy mud under that," Geoffrey answered. "We couldn't get through."

"I reckon I can," the man said confidently. "I'll give it a try anyway." His wagon was pulled by two plodding horses with great feet and rippling muscles.

They lumbered forward, keeping a steady pace, and pulled the wagon through without trouble.

The second wagon, top-heavy with boxes, crates, and furniture, drew level with them. Sitting on the high seat in the front of the wagon were a man and woman. The woman did not even glance down, but stared straight ahead into the prairie wind, her face carved out of stone.

"It's that Mrs. Beattie that was in the boat," Elspeth whispered to Robbie. "You remember her, don't you? She looked after you when you were sick that night."

Robbie was more interested in the calf tethered to their wagon and wanted to pet it, but Elspeth wouldn't let him.

The Beatties' wagon traveled only a little way out into the slough before getting stuck. The straining horses could pull it no farther. There was nothing to do but lighten the load. Mrs. Beattie, holding her skirts above her ankles, splashed back through the mud and settled herself on a box to wait. She watched expressionlessly while Mr. Beattie, helped by men from other wagons, carried crates and furniture and piled them all around her.

"You're going to have to leave some of this here," one of the men said. "There are a lot of these sloughs to cross, and you'll be getting mired down every time with this load."

"Leave one piece behind and I stay here with it," Mrs. Beattie said tonelessly. They must have believed her, for they said nothing more, but continued to work.

The horses were finally able to move the Beatties' wagon, but then boxes and chests had to be unloaded on the other side so that Mr. Beattie could fetch his wife and the rest of their belongings. Geoffrey and Arthur both helped. Mr. Beattie nervously wiped sweat from his forehead and neck, mumbling apologies for the trouble he was causing. He was more than eager to hitch one of his big horses to Geoffrey's cart and pull it through.

It took the entire afternoon to get all the wagons across, and would have taken longer without William Reed and his big horses. "You'll travel with us," he said to Geoffrey, when they were resting between loads.

"We'd be glad to," answered Geoffrey. "Especially through country like this."

At first, Elspeth was sorry to learn that they were joining up with the wagon train. She had enjoyed being on their own. More people would mean more questions. And that Mrs. Beattie, although she never asked anything, and mostly stared straight ahead, sometimes watched Robbie with the strangest expression on her face.

The only other woman in the group was Violet Simms, a young bride, only a few years older than Elspeth. She was obviously glad of company. She came over to sit beside Elspeth while they were waiting for the last of the wagons to cross.

"Are these your brothers?" she asked.

"The little one, Robbie, is my brother," Elspeth answered. "We're just riding with the Whitcombs. We're looking for our aunt and uncle."

"I didn't think he was your brother," Violet said, pointing to Geoffrey. "He talks posh—a bit like the Farthingtons I used to work for in London. But what do you mean, *looking for* your aunt and uncle?"

If Elspeth had known Violet better she might have told her the whole story, but she let the moment pass. She merely said, "We're going to meet them in Battleford. They came out earlier."

"And you came on your own? How old are you anyway?"

"Nearly fourteen," said Elspeth. "I want to get a job as a maid."

"Then you've come to the wrong place, haven't you? If it's a maid's job you're looking for, London's the place. I worked there as a maid myself for Mrs. Farthington. A big, fancy house, she had, with three maids and a cook. Sidney was the groom—that's how he's so good with horses—and we've only been married a month. You should have heard what Netty and Elsie had to say—they were the other maids— when I told them we were going to be big landowners out here! A hundred and sixty acres, and I'll be mistress of my own home!" Violet tossed her black curls.

Elspeth listened, envying the certainty with which Violet faced the future in this vast new land.

# 9

## "Obstacles are something to be overcome"

### APRIL 20–24

THE FOLLOWING MORNING, ELSPETH AND VIOLET were sitting on the high front seat of the Simmses' wagon. Robbie was perched between them, his legs swinging as the wagon jolted along. Sidney was leading Beauty, and Violet had asked Elspeth to ride with her because she wanted someone to talk to.

"That Mrs. Beattie's a funny one," Violet said. "When I try to talk to her, she doesn't even let on I'm there. She puts me in mind of Mrs. Rogers, our cook. Ever so stuck-up, she could be."

Elspeth had been thinking about Mrs. Beattie too. Last night, before they went to bed, when Sidney was playing his fiddle by the campfire, Robbie began dancing, showing off. He was trying to do the Highland fling, the way he used to do it to make Papa laugh, and it had hurt Elspeth to watch him. Then she had noticed Mrs. Beattie looking at Robbie in her strange, hungry way. Elspeth had grabbed him and pulled him down beside her, saying, "Stop acting so silly, Robbie MacDonald. Sit here quiet beside me!" Sidney had said not to spoil the lad's fun, and Robbie had fussed and cried until Elspeth had to bribe him to be quiet with the last piece of barley sugar. All the time, Mrs. Beattie was watching them.

Then, that morning, when they had been getting ready to leave, Robbie had wandered over and patted the Beatties' calf. Elspeth had seen Mrs. Beattie walking toward Robbie, so she had left the dishes and had run over to Robbie, jerking him away from the calf.

"You leave her things alone, do you hear me?"

"I was just talking to it," Robbie said, taken aback to find Elspeth so angry.

"Well, you're not to," Elspeth answered. Robbie began to cry, and although Elspeth knew she was being unfair, she slapped him, telling him to be quiet. Of course, that only made him cry louder, and all the time Elspeth could feel Mrs. Beattie's gaze fixed on both of them.

But now the Beatties' wagon was some distance ahead, so Elspeth put Mrs. Beattie out of her mind and listened to Violet talking about her wedding day, and about the cake that Mrs. Rogers had made.

"Ever so pretty, it was, all decorated with violets and forget-me-nots—because of my name, see? Netty didn't eat her piece. She put it under her pillow so she'd dream about the man she's going to marry. I wonder if she's found him yet!"

Elspeth loved listening to Violet's chatter, and Violet enjoyed having an audience. The only problem was that Violet didn't have much patience with Robbie, and he didn't care one bit about the affairs of the Farthington household. He kept interrupting, asking if he could get down and walk.

"Let Arthur and Geoffrey take him for a bit," Violet suggested. "There's not really enough room for him here. Or let him walk if he wants to."

"He'd get too far behind," Elspeth answered. "I'd have to walk with him."

"Please yourself," said Violet with a shrug. "Seems to me you fuss about him too much."

Elspeth felt annoyed with Violet. After all, Robbie was only four years old and needed someone to look after him.

She was about to jump down from the wagon when Sidney shouted up to Robbie, "Do you want to ride on Beauty, lad?"

Robbie didn't need a second invitation. He was soon sitting happily on Beauty's broad back, his fingers tangled in her mane. Pig-Bear was buttoned in his jacket, his head sticking out so that he could warn them if he saw Indians. Robbie and Sidney discussed Indians at length.

On the fourth day, they reached Eagle Creek. They had all heard plenty of hair-raising stories about this particular crossing, yet they stood in a huddled group, staring with disbelief at the narrow trail twisting down one side of the gully and up the other like a carelessly tossed brown ribbon. At the bottom, almost within reach of the swirling brown waters of the creek, lay the matchwood remains of a broken wagon.

"There should be a bridge," Violet said. "We can't cross that. I don't think we're even on the right road."

"Have you seen any other?" Geoffrey asked.

"London was never like this!" Sidney said, shaking his head.

Finally, William Reed said that they would need to jam poles between the spokes of the back wheels of the wagons to keep them from outrunning the horses on the way down. Cottonwood trees grew thick in the gully, so some of the men scrambled down to cut and trim poles.

"I reckon I'll have a go at it," Reed volunteered when they had the wagons ready. No one challenged his right to go first. "I don't like the way the land's slipping on these sharp turns, but I'm sure that if there was a safer place to cross, someone would have found it," he added.

Elspeth and Robbie sat quietly at the top of the ravine, watching each outfit descend the treacherous path. Reed's wagon slithered at the first bend, but after that he had no real trouble. The Beatties' wagon, top-heavy with their belongings, took the first turn all right, but at the second bend, one wheel hung over the edge for a moment, causing the wagon to lurch and the load to shift. Mrs. Beattie, sitting up front as erect as ever, was the only one who did not cheer with relief when the wagon righted itself with no harm done. Poor Mr. Beattie, straining at the reins, had sweat streaming down his white face. He was so exhausted when he reached the bottom that

William Reed had to lift him down from the wagon.

"You'd better walk down with Robbie," Arthur said to Elspeth.

Violet would have liked to walk with them, but Sidney needed her to help with their wagon. She was so frightened that Elspeth didn't think she'd be much help. But the Simmses and the Whitcombs both had smaller outfits than most and managed better.

When they had all reached the bottom, they faced the new hazard of crossing the creek, swollen at this time of year by spring rains and melting snow. It was here that the bigger wagons had an advantage. Geoffrey was worried about a back wheel that was wobbling a little, but decided to try to reach the top of the gully before they did anything about it.

"Maybe you and Robbie had better cross with Sidney," he said to Elspeth. "I don't want you thrown into the river if the axle breaks."

Violet was only too glad of company. "I can't swim," she said. "So if this thing tips over, I'm going to hang on to you!"

"Don't do that!" said Elspeth. "I can't swim either. You'd do better to hold on to a wooden crate."

They all watched each wagon in turn ease into the swirling water as if their collective wills could guide the horses safely to the other side. When the Simmses' turn came, Robbie clung to Elspeth, half fearful and half fascinated by the water rising almost to the top of the wheel. Then it seemed to fall away as Beauty dragged the wagon onto the narrow strip of shingle on the other side.

They jumped down and ran to the water's edge to shout encouragement to Geoffrey and Arthur, who were now almost halfway across. The water was even higher on their small cart. Suddenly, the right front wheel plunged into a hole, the cart swayed, and something went flying from the top of the luggage in a wide arc and landed in the river.

"It's Pig-Bear! It's Pig-Bear!" Robbie screamed. "It's Pig-Bear and he's drowning!"

Elspeth, afraid that Robbie was going to jump in after Pig-Bear, went running alongside the creek, trying to keep the poor battered toy, swirling and bobbing in the brown, frothy water, in sight. At the first bend, she tripped over a root and plunged right into the river. Her breath left her completely as she felt the icy water rush over her, roaring in her ears and tearing at her clothes. She tried frantically to struggle back to the shore, but she was completely at the mercy of the rushing water, caught in the swirling current. For a long, sickening moment she could not feel the gravel bottom with her feet, but her knee hit sharply against a rock, and she felt herself being dragged across stones. The rushing sound of the water was replaced by voices—crying, screaming, shouting voices. Someone was shaking her, calling her name.

"Of all the stupid things to do! To jump in after that silly animal!" Arthur was saying, shaking her by the shoulders so that her hair slapped wetly against her cheeks. "Do you never think before you do anything?"

"Why did you dive in when you couldn't swim?" Violet asked.

"I fell," Elspeth explained, but no one listened. No one could hear above the noise of the creek and Robbie's crying. He went on crying even though someone had rescued Pig-Bear from where it had become entangled with the branches of a cottonwood tree trailing in the swollen water.

"I thought you were drownded," Robbie said to Elspeth, tears streaming down his face.

"I knew it would be like this, taking children with us," Geoffrey said in a disgusted voice, turning his back on Elspeth.

"We'd better get the rest of the wagons up top while there's still light," William Reed suggested. The incident was all but forgotten as they turned to face new problems.

Elspeth didn't wait for Arthur or Violet to offer her a ride, but trudged up the steep slope from the creek bottom. Robbie reached for her hand, but she ignored him. He followed her quietly. Elspeth's wet clothes clung to her, and the wind, razor keen, took her breath away. By the time they reached the top her jaws ached from chattering and she could hardly claw her way up the last few yards. But even worse than the numbing cold was the memory of the sharp, angry voices shouting at her as they dragged her from the river. They had shouted at her more to release their own tension than in anger, the way she often did with Robbie. But Elspeth felt that the closeness, the feeling of belonging, was gone. Geoffrey's taunt about taking children with them rang in her ears.

She stood shivering, as near the fire as possible, but still she could not get warm. It was a smoky fire of wet, green cottonwood, and did not give off much heat. She had changed out of her wet outer clothes and spread her coat to dry, but foolishly she had not taken off the gray skirt, which still clung damply to her legs. She had worn it night and day, ever since she left Scotland, and only felt safe as long as she could feel the money sewn in the lining of the bodice. She shivered again and tried to get closer to the fire, but the thick smoke made her eyes smart.

The sky was gray and heavy and seemed to merge in the distance with the gray land. As darkness fell, snow dusted the ground, and the wind howled with a new note. Elspeth and Robbie slept in one of the government tents that night. It offered more protection than the tarpaulin, but Elspeth was still cold and slept fitfully.

Snow continued to blow in the wind all the next day. Elspeth huddled with Robbie in the back of Arthur's cart. She hadn't the energy to listen to Violet's chatter. Thinking that it might help the stiffness in her joints and muscles, she forced herself to walk for a while. All the time she wondered how the world could have changed so suddenly. The emptiness of the land made her feel puny now, not important; the long, straight trail surely led nowhere; the wind carried threats, not promises.

She tried to think about what she was going to do when she got to Battleford. She would ask Arthur to take them to the hotel. Suppose there wasn't a hotel? There must, at least, be a boardinghouse. She stumbled and then dragged herself back to the cart. She'd have to act surprised when Uncle Donald and Aunt Maud weren't there. She'd show the Whitcombs that she had money for a room. Then she'd wait for news of Mr. Barr. He'd help her. He'd look after her . . . wasn't that what he'd said on the ship? . . . that he was responsible for all these people. . . .

In her head she carried on an imaginary conversation with Mr. Barr, but sometimes she seemed to be talking to Uncle Donald and sometimes even to Papa. If only Papa were here to look after them. . . .

That night, in their tent, Elspeth counted out the money for the hotel. They'd likely want to see her money before they rented her a room. Everyone looked shabby and dirty and weary, but she realized that she and Rob looked worse than most. She would have liked to offer some money to Arthur, because she knew he was worried about being short of supplies for the rest of the journey, but he had been so aloof since Eagle Creek.

The next day, Elspeth coughed and was feverish. She had given up the idea that exercise would help her aches and pains. When she had tried to walk, the ground swayed in an alarming way, and the flat prairie seemed to be all uphill. It took all her strength to cling to the jolting cart.

Robbie sat close beside her, a Shadow Bairn again, whispering words of comfort. "Arthur says we'll soon be seeing Uncle Donald and Aunt Maud." Getting no response from Elspeth, he said, "Arthur says Uncle Donald'll give me a wee calf of my own. He's sure he will. It can be yours, too, Elspeth. . . . It would be nice to have milk again, wouldn't it? Talk to me, Elspeth!"

Elspeth hardly knew they had reached Battleford, although the rest of the group was wildly excited to see the houses and stores and mills at the meeting place of the Battle and Saskatchewan rivers. This would be their last chance to buy provisions and send messages back home before pressing on to find their own land. There was an air of urgency, almost as if they were nearing the end of a long race. The land was waiting, and the best claims would go to those who got there first. Even Sidney Simms, who had never been outside London before, could see that there were stretches of this land that could never be tamed by a plow.

"You'll want to go to the hotel," Arthur said to Elspeth. "I do hope your uncle and aunt are there."

Arthur's voice sounded unnecessarily loud. What was he saying? Oh, yes! Uncle Donald and Aunt Maud—they were waiting for them at a hotel. It would be nice to have someone to look after Robbie for her. And it would be nice to have someone to look after her.

"Are you all right?" Arthur asked anxiously.

"I'm just tired," said Elspeth.

The cart jolted to a stop again. A building—a hotel? Robbie was shouting that Aunt Maud and Uncle Donald were going to meet them there. Elspeth nodded in agreement. Yes, they had money for a room. She had the money here in her hand—lucky she'd thought of that last night. Could she go to the room now? To lie down . . . to sleep . . . till Aunt Maud came. . . .

A girl, not much older than Elspeth, was saying something to Arthur, and Elspeth forced herself to make sense of the words.

"Mrs. Morgan's not here just now," the girl was saying. "She'd be the one who would know about their uncle and aunt. MacDonald, you said the name was? She hasn't mentioned them to me."

"When will Mrs. Morgan be back?" Arthur asked.

"Less than an hour, I should think. Will *you* be wanting a room?"

"Not likely!" said Arthur with a bitter laugh. "We've no money for hotels. We're not even stopping in Battleford for supplies. We have to push on. My brother's waiting outside."

Everything in the hotel lobby where they were standing was swimming before Elspeth's eyes. A huge Chinese vase seemed to topple from its stand, but miraculously never reached the floor; when Elspeth focussed on it again, it was back where it belonged.

Arthur was asking again if she'd be all right here until her relatives turned up. She must have found words to reassure him, because he finally left, and then the maid showed her and Robbie through to a small room at the back of the hotel. Elspeth lay down on the narrow bed and slept.

# 10

## "Not seldom privations"

### APRIL 29

ELSPETH OPENED HER EYES SLOWLY AND LOOKED around, wondering where she was. The room was narrow, bare of furniture except for a wooden chair and a spindly table on which stood a cracked pitcher and washbowl. Bright sunlight poured through the small window. Her traveling bag was sitting in one corner.

It was the sight of the battered leather bag that brought back the memory of the journey—the boat, the train, and then the wagon ride to Battleford. And when they got to Battleford, Uncle Donald had been there—and he'd slammed the door when they tried to get in. Or had that been a dream?

She struggled to separate the dream from reality, but the picture of Uncle Donald was so vivid that she was sure he'd really been here in the room.

Where was Robbie? He had cried, wanting supper, and she had nothing to give him. Then someone had come in, someone she knew, and had kept asking if she understood. She had been glad when they went away. And Mr. Barr had been there, talking to her.

He'd said he would help her—or had that been a dream too?

So much remembering tired her. She drifted off to sleep again. The next time she awakened, there was a man sitting on the chair beside the bed. He was dressed in black, and he had a small black beard like a fringe around his chin. Elspeth tried to ask him who he was, but her words were thick and jumbled.

He seemed to understand, though, because he leaned over her, saying, "I'm Dr. Wallace. I'm going to give you some more medicine to make you sleep." His eyes were blue and kind.

Papa's eyes were blue. . . .

When Elspeth woke again, the man was gone. She wondered if he had really been there, or if he was just another dream person like Uncle Donald and Isaac Barr. Or maybe she had talked to them too. And where was Robbie?

The room was very hot. The blankets felt heavy, so Elspeth pushed them back. Suddenly she was wide awake, struggling to sit up. What was this that she was wearing? A white nightgown with a lace collar. Where was her skirt with the bodice? Where was her money?

With her breath coming in short gasps, Elspeth crawled across the room to the traveling bag. Shakily she sorted through her belongings. The skirt wasn't there. She dragged herself back to bed. As she lay down her mind raced, all her thoughts suddenly in sharp focus. The discovery that the money was gone erased the dulling effect of her sickness and the medicine. With painful clarity, she recalled everything from the day of Papa's death. . . .

"Robbie! Robbie!" Her voice sounded weak and strange in her ears.

The door opened. Elspeth turned toward it eagerly, but it was not Robbie who came into the room. A tall woman with upswept hair paused in the doorway and then crossed over to the bed, her blue silk dress rustling as she walked. There was something about her disinterested expression, even when she inquired if Elspeth were feeling better, that reminded Elspeth of the social worker in Glasgow. Elspeth labeled her as one of *them* and drew farther down under the covers.

"Well?" the woman asked, waiting for Elspeth to speak.

"Where's Robbie?"

"Is that still all you can say?"

"Where *is* Robbie?" Elspeth asked, raising herself on her elbow.

"No one has seen this Robbie you keep asking for—or your Uncle Donald and Aunt Maud. What we want to know is, who are *you* and what are you doing here?"

"I'm Elspeth MacDonald," she answered weakly. "I came here with Robbie to find—to find—Mr. Barr."

"Mr. Barr? Isaac Barr? What business could *you* have with Isaac Barr?"

"I was hoping he'd help me."

"I don't know what help you expect to get from

him, but you've missed him anyway. He was here last night and left this morning."

He was here last night. Then *had* he been in her room—or was it a dream?

"He's gone up to the colony to sort things out if he can," the woman continued. "He promised land to people on the boat, but then he didn't register the claims, and now other people have settled these sections. They say, too, that he's been making a good profit for himself on supplies he sells through the syndicate—money that should go to the company. But I'll say this for Isaac Barr. He's been good for business. Every room in the hotel has been full for days. And here you are, taking up a room! What guarantee do I have that this uncle and aunt of yours are going to pay?"

"*I* paid for the room! I paid the girl at the door, and I can pay the rest when I get my skirt back."

"I know nothing about you paying. And what does your skirt have to do with it?"

"But where's Robbie?" Elspeth asked distractedly. "He's four years old and has fair hair."

"There's been no four-year-old around here. He'll have gone on with your aunt and uncle."

"He's here somewhere," Elspeth insisted. "He must be hiding."

"For five days?" the woman asked.

"Have I been ill for five days?" Elspeth whispered in a frightened voice.

"Five days—as sure as my name's Kate Morgan! Dr. Wallace has been coming in twice a day, sometimes more. A fine thing, your aunt and uncle just leaving you here like this."

"But they didn't leave me!" said Elspeth. "I'm alone, except for Robbie."

It took Mrs. Morgan some time to grasp that Elspeth had not been left behind by her aunt and uncle and that there was no way that Robbie could be with them. "We thought, maybe, your aunt and uncle didn't want to lose time waiting for you to get better," Mrs. Morgan said. "Everyone's in such a rush to get up there. Goodness knows what they expect to find! But I still don't see how you got here alone—and with a little brother!"

Shaking her head, Mrs. Morgan went off to fetch Dr. Wallace, sure that the sickness had muddled the girl's mind.

Dr. Wallace came to the hotel right away. Kate Morgan had been none too pleased when he had told her, on his first visit, that the child couldn't be moved. Mrs. Morgan had made it clear that she wasn't going to take on the role of nurse. She already had all she could do, with the hotel full, and her stepdaughter, Peg, going off without a word to anyone. At first Mrs. Morgan had been afraid that Elspeth had scarlet fever (there were rumored to be cases in Saskatoon), but Dr. Wallace had reassured her about that. He, himself, had wondered if he would pull the child through. She was poor and undernourished, but she did seem to have a core of inner strength that gave him reason to hope.

When Dr. Wallace walked into her bedroom,

Elspeth recognized him at once by his shiny black suit and trim black beard. "Do you know where Robbie is?" she asked, for that was all that mattered to her now.

Sitting down on the chair beside the bed, Dr. Wallace said, "You've been talking a lot about this Robbie, and about your aunt and uncle. Even about Isaac Barr. But I still haven't been able to piece your story together."

"Where *is* Robbie?" Elspeth asked again.

"I can't help you find him until you tell me more. Why don't you begin at the beginning?"

The doctor listened to Elspeth's soft Scottish voice as she told of Papa and Mama and Robbie in Glasgow, of her father's dream of owning his own land and of how Isaac Barr had promised to make that dream come true. She spoke, falteringly, of her parents' deaths, and of the social worker coming and wanting to take Robbie from her.

"So you ran away," Dr. Wallace said quietly. "I ran away from Scotland too." Then he added, as much to himself as to Elspeth, "Megan must be twelve years old now. Leaving childhood behind and becoming a woman. I wonder if she's like her mother. Her mother—Jeannie Wallace—was my wife."

Elspeth wasn't really listening. She was thinking about Robbie. Was he still a Shadow Bairn? She began to tell the doctor about how they had been Shadow Bairns and hid from *them* on the boat, about talking to Isaac Barr, and about the long train ride to

Saskatoon. He felt her frustration when the immigration men would not listen, and her contentment on the trail to Battleford; but all the time he was remembering Jeannie Wallace and how she had died in childbirth with him beside her. He might have saved her and not the child, but in saving the child he lost Jeannie. He lost them both, for he gave the baby, Megan, to Jeannie's mother to rear, and came out to Canada. He had never been back.

"I've got to find Robbie," Elspeth was saying, a frantic edge to her voice. "And I've got to find my money—the money in my skirt! This isn't my nightgown, you know."

"It's what you were wearing when Mrs. Morgan called me in to see you."

"Then Mrs. Morgan must have stolen my money."

"I don't believe that," Dr. Wallace answered. "She wasn't any too pleased to find you here, but she didn't take your money."

"Then the girl did! The girl who rented me the room."

"Peg? Peg has moved out—probably up to the colony," said Dr. Wallace thoughtfully. "But there's nothing to prove that you had money, is there?"

"Arthur knew, because I paid him to bring us here," Elspeth said.

"Arthur knew? And where's he now?" Dr. Wallace asked sharply. "He left you here, knowing that you were sick?"

"I don't think he realized I was sick," said Elspeth. "And he didn't steal any money."

"Could Robbie be with him?"

"Maybe he is," said Elspeth slowly. With her gray eyes wide and pleading, she added, "You will help me find him, won't you? Everything I've done was to keep us together. I can't go on without him."

The doctor looked at Elspeth's thin, eager face. "How old are you?" he asked abruptly.

"I'm thirteen, nearly fourteen," Elspeth answered. "When I find Robbie, I'm going to get a job somewhere so that we can be together. I thought maybe I could work as a maid, or in a hotel."

"I'll look for Robbie," Dr. Wallace said at last. "But when I find him, I think you should go back to Scotland. Life is too hard, too uncertain, for you here on your own."

"No! We can't go back," Elspeth said earnestly. "But please, please find Robbie."

"You'll have to tell me again about the people you traveled with from Saskatoon, and anyone else who might have befriended him."

"But if he's with someone I know, then why haven't they brought him back?" Elspeth asked.

"There hasn't been time," Dr. Wallace pointed out. "The way the weather has been, they'll not have reached the colony yet. It's a three-day ride in good weather. And it takes time to choose land and register a claim. It will be weeks before they have a chance to get back here. But are you sure no one told you they were taking him?"

"Sometimes I think there was someone . . . but I only remember Uncle Donald . . . and that must have been a dream. Yet someone came." The memory tortured Elspeth, and was to haunt her for weeks.

Dr. Wallace, thinking back to how ill she had been, realized that there was little point in pressing her.

During the week that followed, Elspeth wondered impatiently when Dr. Wallace was going to start looking for Robbie. She didn't know that he was already making inquiries around Battleford. It puzzled him that no one had seen the boy in the town or in the hotel. Sometimes he asked himself how he had got so involved in this girl's affairs. He even found himself planting the idea in Kate Morgan's mind that Elspeth could wash dishes in the hotel in exchange for her room and board while he was gone. That way she'd have somewhere to stay.

"She hardly looks strong enough," Kate Morgan answered. "Keeping a place like this going is hard work."

"I'm sure it is," the doctor agreed. "But there must be something she could do. It would keep her mind off Robbie."

"You really fell for that story, didn't you?" said Mrs. Morgan with a sniff. "If you ask me, it's nothing but lies! What's she doing coming here when her aunt and uncle are in Manitoba? And all this nonsense about someone stealing her money!"

However, Mrs. Morgan did give Elspeth a job. She grudgingly admitted to Dr. Wallace, before he left for the colony, that Elspeth was a willing worker and didn't spend all her time in front of the mirror the way Peg used to do.

When Dr. Wallace rode away, Elspeth's hands were busy—washing dishes, peeling potatoes, making beds—but her thoughts were with the doctor. Would he find Robbie with Arthur and Geoffrey? She remembered saying good-bye to Arthur in the hall. She was sure that Robbie had been with her after that. He had cried in their room, and then someone had taken him away. Someone she knew. But all that remained in her mind was a shadow, a distorted shadow in a dream. Sometimes, especially in the lonely hours of the night, she imagined that the immigration man had taken Robbie and sent him back to Scotland, leaving her here alone as a punishment for deceiving him. But Robbie wouldn't have gone with the immigration man. He knew that the immigration man was one of *them*. Robbie *had* to be with Arthur or Violet. Dr. Wallace would find him.

# 11

## "More or less of hardship"

### MAY

AFTER NEARLY TWELVE YEARS IN THE SASKATCHEWAN country, Dr. Wallace knew the prairie well enough not to fear it, yet he could appreciate the effect of these vast open spaces on the newly arrived settlers. They were people accustomed to bustling towns and cozy villages, people accustomed to walls and fences and hills and trees, people accustomed to people.

Dr. Wallace's destination was Headquarter's Camp on the Fourth Meridian. In the land agent's office he met William Reed, who dispelled any lingering worry the doctor had that there was no such person as Robbie.

"That lad had a way with animals," the big farmer said slowly. "He had no fear in him. He'd walk right up to my Clydesdale horses and feed them a handful of grass. A sharp little fellow, but too young to look after himself if he has wandered out there somewhere on the prairie."

"You haven't seen him since you left Battleford?" Dr. Wallace asked.

William Reed shook his head. "Not that I remember," he said.

With the help of directions from the land agent, Dr. Wallace found the Simmses' claim. Violet was cooking dinner in a small tent. Sidney was struggling to plow his first furrows, although the ground was too wet to work easily. He was going to use the clods of earth turned over by the plow to build their house.

"It isn't what I thought of back at Mrs. Farthington's when I bragged to Elsie that I'd be mistress of my own home," Violet confessed ruefully to Dr. Wallace. "But it's a start, Sidney says. Just till we get money from our first crop."

Violet was terribly upset when she learned the reason for the doctor's visit. But with Sidney busy plowing, and their nearest neighbor more than a mile away, she was hungering for someone to talk to. Dr. Wallace soon formed a clear picture of the boy he was looking for. A friendly little chap, with tousled hair and shabby clothes, who chewed on an old toy.

"He used to sit up there on Beauty's back looking out for Indians, with that ragged Pig-Bear of his," Violet said. "You don't suppose the Indians have him, do you? He was awfully interested in them. Not frightened, just interested. He'd have gone with them if they had asked him."

Violet had not seen Robbie since Battleford. She didn't know much about the others who had traveled with them in the wagon train from Saskatoon to Battleford either. They had all gone their separate ways. Some had spent a few days in Battleford resting and buying new provisions. Others had gone directly to the colony.

When Sidney came in from his plowing, Violet invited Dr. Wallace to stay for dinner. Over the meal, he listened to Sidney talk about the land he was going to plow and the crops he was going to grow.

"It's like Barr says—there's wealth in this land!" Sidney said eagerly. "London was never like this!"

Dr. Wallace didn't know whether to be impressed by the young man's enthusiasm or amused by his innocence.

The following day, Dr. Wallace rode down to the Beatties' claim, which was in an isolated area near the southern boundary of the colony. They had chosen good land, and already had the beginnings of a barn. Beside their tent was a great pile of crates and furniture, covered over by a tarpaulin.

"Anybody here?" Dr. Wallace shouted.

A woman emerged from the tent. One look at her hard, unresponsive face made the doctor think that perhaps it was the isolation and not the good land that had drawn her to this place.

"Mrs. Beattie?"

She nodded.

"I'm making enquiries about a lost boy, Robbie MacDonald. He traveled from Saskatoon with the Whitcomb brothers."

She stared at him resentfully and said nothing.

"Where's your husband?" Dr. Wallace asked. "Maybe he'd know something."

"About a lost bairn? Not him! He's away buying

lumber for the house. I'll be glad when he gets started on it. Do you see what the rain is doing to my furniture?"

"There's plenty of people having to get along without furniture," Dr. Wallace said.

"Aye! Because they didn't have the foresight to bring it with them." Mrs. Beattie sniffed.

"Did you ever hear anything about the girl Elspeth MacDonald having money with her?" Dr. Wallace asked.

"She had no money," Mrs. Beattie answered. "They were penniless bairns going out to live on the charity of relatives."

"They weren't going out to relatives. They do have an uncle and aunt in Manitoba, but they knew nothing about the children coming."

"No Uncle Donald and Aunt Maud?" Mrs. Beattie asked, apparently surprised.

"You've heard of them?" Dr. Wallace asked sharply.

"Just that the children spoke of this aunt and uncle as if they were meeting them in Battleford."

"That was wishful thinking, poor souls!"

"You say the boy is lost. What about the girl?"

"She's working in the hotel in Battleford. It's the lad I want to find."

A sharp, heavy shower brought their interview to a close. Mrs. Beattie ran over to anchor down a corner of the tarpaulin that was blowing loose, and Dr. Wallace got back on his horse. He could have done with a hot meal, or even a cup of tea, but the idea of prairie hospitality didn't seem to have spread to the Beatties.

Back at Headquarters Camp, Dr. Wallace felt discouraged. The only people left to interview who had known Robbie well were the Whitcomb brothers, but there was little likelihood that Robbie was with them. Apparently they had not had enough money between them to pay the ten-dollar filing fee on a claim, so they were doing odd jobs for other settlers. No one knew where they were working now.

Still, the doctor's time wasn't wasted while he was trying to locate the Whitcombs. He had been urged to set up surgery in a tent, even if just for a few days, to take care of some of the emergencies that had arisen. There had been a rash of accidents—cuts from carelessly used axes and crushed limbs from falling logs. Dr. Wallace had a steady stream of patients.

Late on the second afternoon, the doctor looked up to see a young man limping in. Another gashed leg from chopping wood.

"What's your name?" Dr. Wallace asked.

"Arthur Whitcomb."

"The very person I've been looking for!"

Arthur flinched as the doctor ripped off the dirty bandage. "Why are you looking for me?" he asked.

"What do you know about the MacDonald children?"

"We gave them a ride to Battleford. They're all right, I hope."

"The boy is missing."

"Robbie? Isn't he with the uncle? Donald Mac-Donald, who was meeting them in Battleford."

"Their only uncle is in Manitoba."

"Then why were they going to Battleford?" Arthur sounded genuinely puzzled.

"To escape the immigration people. I understand that they paid you to take them along."

Arthur squirmed, but it could have been from pain. Dr. Wallace was cleaning the wound. "We needed the money. We couldn't have paid for the pony and cart without it. And they wanted to get out of Saskatoon."

"Do you know if she had more money?"

Arthur shook his head.

"She says she's lost nearly eighty pounds. She claims someone stole it."

"I don't know what you're getting at," Arthur said abruptly. "But I'd say finding the boy is more important than the money. And where's Elspeth now?"

"She's working in the Battleford hotel. She was very sick when she first got there. It was then that Robbie was taken or ran off."

"I thought, maybe, she was sick."

"Then why did you leave her?" the doctor asked.

"What could we do? We had no money and no place to take her, and her uncle was supposed to be coming. Besides, we were in a hurry to get up here. God knows why!"

"You haven't got land yet?"

"We never seem to get enough money together. This place runs on a barter system, but you can't pay a filing fee with a pound of butter and a dozen eggs."

The doctor pulled a crumpled bill from his pocket and said, "Get down there today and claim your land. You need something of your own that you believe in to survive in this country."

"But I—I should be paying you," Arthur stammered. "Not the other way around!"

"I don't like to see you beaten before you start," said the doctor gruffly. "Get along, and learn how to use an ax!"

Dr. Wallace watched Arthur go, then turned down the paraffin lamp. What was the matter with him? he wondered, getting involved in his patients' lives like this. For twelve years he had lived alone, mostly among men who wanted to be left alone, but that was all changing. The country was being overrun by lads who didn't know the sharp edge of an ax and girls hardly older than his own daughter. Maybe he should move on—or maybe it was time to go back to Scotland. . . . But first, he wished he could find Robbie MacDonald.

Could there be a connection between Peg, the money, and the boy? the doctor wondered. They had all disappeared at the same time. From what he'd seen of Peg Morgan, she might easily have been tempted by the money, but she wouldn't have taken on the responsibility of a four-year-old boy. It was the older lads she had an eye for. But his attempts to trace Peg came to nothing. She had vanished as completely as Robbie.

In the end he returned to Battleford, defeated.

Elspeth was in the hotel kitchen washing dishes when Dr. Wallace broke the news that he hadn't found Robbie. She turned away from him, staring out the window. Across the flat land behind the hotel was a stand of willows clothed in bright spring green, and beyond the willows, the glint of the river, reflecting the red evening sky.

"You don't suppose—you don't think—the river. . . ."

"I just don't know," Dr. Wallace answered in a tired voice. "The lad could have wandered there unnoticed that evening. I think you should go away from here—maybe even back to Scotland. I've been thinking—"

Elspeth turned on him, her eyes blazing with anger. "That's all you can say! Go back to Scotland! Back to Scotland so that you can forget about me and my troubles! Well, I'm not going! I'm going to stay right here till Robbie comes back, because this is where he'll expect to find me."

It was her determination that Dr. Wallace admired most.

# 12

## "Hard work and plenty of it"

### JUNE

ELSPETH TURNED FOURTEEN IN THE MIDDLE OF JUNE, and almost overnight she seemed to grow up. The brown dress was so short and shabby that Mrs. Morgan, complaining that Elspeth was hardly fit to be seen in such a rag, found her a dress that Peg had outgrown. It was dark green calico with tiny white buttons from the collar to the waist and matching buttons on the cuffs.

Yet it wasn't the dress that made Elspeth look older. It was more the expression in her eyes. After Papa's and Mama's deaths, she still had something to hold on to—Papa's dream and her own promise to Mama to look after Robbie. With Robbie gone, she had failed them all. The empty ache of missing him was always there. The sound of a child's voice crying in one of the rooms, or the sight of a tousled blond head, brought with it a surge of hope that was followed by the agony of loss all over again.

She lived from day to day, waiting on tables, making beds, washing dishes. Occasionally Mrs.

Morgan sent her down to the store, but Elspeth took no interest in the raw, bustling town. The stores were crowded, and the lumber mills were doing brisk business, but Elspeth caught none of the excitement.

Mrs. Morgan soon took Elspeth's presence for granted. The girl worked hard and kept to herself, and that was how Mrs. Morgan felt it should be. The only person who took an interest in Elspeth was Dr. Wallace. He used to drop in at the hotel sometimes. But there was a constraint between them now. He felt that he had failed Elspeth by not finding Robbie, while she found his kindness harder to bear than other people's indifference.

One afternoon when she was dusting the tall Chinese vase in the hall, she heard shrill voices on the stair above her. "Elspeth! Elspeth! What are *you* doing here?"

Elspeth looked up and saw two girls running down the stairs, pushing each other in their eagerness to reach her. She knew them at once, although they no longer had their jaunty braids. But they still looked exactly alike. Their heads were covered with a soft fuzz of orange-red hair, cut shorter than any boy's.

Rebecca covered her head with her hands, saying, "Isn't it awful? They cut it all off! We were sick, and they cut off our hair."

"We had scarlet fever," Rachel explained. "We had to stay in Saskatoon with Mama for weeks, and nobody could come near us. Papa and Matthew went on up to the colony to claim land."

"They're coming here to get us," Rachel said.

Rebecca interrupted to tell about the house that Papa had built for them.

"Where's Robbie? Where's Robbie?" Rachel wanted to know.

Rebecca, looking gleefully down the shadowy hallway, asked, "Can we play Shadow Bairns again?"

The girls' voices trailed off as they looked up at Elspeth's face—the white, strained face of a stranger.

"Robbie's not here," Elspeth said. "I've lost him."

"Did *they* get him?" Rebecca asked in a hushed whisper.

Elspeth sank down on the bottom step of the stairs, her head leaning against the smooth wood of the newel post, and began to sob, deep tearing sobs that wracked her thin body. A frightened, questioning look passed between Rachel and Rebecca. Tentatively, Rachel put her arm around Elspeth's shaking shoulders, while Rebecca ran back up to their room to fetch Mama.

It took a long time to explain to Mrs. Galbraith about Elspeth and Robbie. Although she had heard about them on the boat, she had been too seasick to follow Rachel's and Rebecca's chatter. The twins had rambled about Elspeth and Robbie and Shadow Bairns when they had scarlet fever, but Mrs. Galbraith thought they were characters in a game, the way Shadow Bairns were.

Gradually, she pieced together the story of the children traveling alone, Elspeth's illness, Robbie's disappearance, and the doctor's search in the colony. It was all incredible. She remembered the ordeal of her own violent sickness and fear on the boat. She couldn't imagine children managing alone.

"What are you doing now?" Mrs. Galbraith asked.

"Waiting for him to come back, ma'am. I'm waiting here for wee Rob."

"But it has been weeks, Elspeth," Mrs. Galbraith said gently.

"Someone took him, you see," Elspeth answered. "I had this dream, so I know he'll come back. I'm waiting for him."

Mrs. Galbraith looked helplessly at Elspeth. What could she say to the child? She wasn't that much older than Rachel and Rebecca. Suppose when they had been ill there had been no one to care for them? She wished her husband were here so that she could discuss the suggestion she was about to make. But surely he would understand.

"I'm expecting a baby soon, Elspeth. I want to get up to the claim to be near John when the baby is born, but sometimes I wonder how I'll manage the work. Would you come and stay with us and help with the girls and the washing and so on?"

Rachel and Rebecca immediately began to plead with Elspeth to come, but their mother told them to be quiet.

"Think it over," she said to Elspeth. "I'm sure it would be no more work than you do here. It will be crowded, though, and I don't know what John's going to say."

"She can sleep with us," Rebecca said eagerly.

Elspeth didn't know what to think about Mrs.

Galbraith's offer. Sometimes she wanted to stay in Battleford, sealed inside the shell of work and the routine that she had built around herself. Here no one made demands of her beyond the household chores. No one tore open her wounds with words like "Remember when . . ." or questions about the future. Here she truly was a Shadow Bairn, unnoticed by the stream of people who passed through the hotel. The Galbraiths would demand more than that.

Their demands started right away. Mrs. Galbraith asked Mrs. Morgan if Elspeth could be spared to take the girls out for a walk on the prairie while she rested. Grudgingly, Mrs. Morgan said that she could go, then reminded Elspeth when she was leaving that there would be sheets to iron when she got back.

The prairie in June was breathtakingly beautiful. White, blue, and yellow flowers sprinkled the ground like confetti, and the wind rippled through the grass so that Elspeth found herself thinking of the dancing waters of Loch Nevis. Then, on a bank near the Battle River, they discovered a huge patch of wild strawberries.

"There must be a million," Rebecca said, falling to her knees and cramming the sweet berries into her mouth.

"We should take some home to Ma," Rachel suggested.

The following afternoon, Mrs. Morgan told Elspeth to run down to the store to buy some lard. Elspeth asked the twins to go with her. Coming from the opposite direction, they saw a crowd of men, two mounted on small ponies, the rest scuffing through the dust in soft moccasins. Black hair hung straight to their shoulders, and they wore ragged, ill-matched clothing.

"Indians!" Rebecca said in a breathless whisper.

When the Indians turned into the store, the children followed them, but Rachel was mortified to find that she and Rebecca were the center of attention. One of the men actually touched her soft orange-red hair, and her head tingled as if the Indian was going to scalp her. She ran outside and across the road. There she waited for Elspeth to come out with her purchases.

"I don't like Indians," she said. "I don't like how they looked at us."

"We were staring at them too," Elspeth pointed out.

"I thought they were going to take us away. Do you think they steal children?"

"Of course not," answered Elspeth.

"Maybe they stole Robbie."

"Don't be silly!" Elspeth said sharply. She wished the twins wouldn't keep reminding her about Robbie, although, to be fair, she had been thinking about him too. How he had always wanted to see Indians. Suppose he had wandered onto the prairie that day and had been found by some passing Indians. Would they bring him back to town? Or would they just keep him?

When the Indians left the store, she followed them to the edge of the town where their woman waited, patiently watching while the children romped and played. Elspeth looked at the children eagerly. They stopped their tumbling about and gazed back at her with bright, black eyes—not a blue pair among them. The Indians filed on to the empty prairie. Elspeth watched them until they were just small dots in the distance, then turned back to the hotel discouraged. With so much land out there, what chance was there of finding one small boy?

That same evening, Dr. Wallace came into the hotel dining room and ordered coffee. "I notice you've found friends," he said to Elspeth, who was clearing tables.

"The Galbraiths want me to go up to the colony with them so that I can help Mrs. Galbraith with the work after the baby comes," Elspeth said. "But I'm not sure if I should go."

"It sounds an ideal arrangement," Dr. Wallace said enthusiastically.

"You'd let me know if Robbie ever came back?" Elspeth asked quietly.

"I might not be here, Elspeth. I've been thinking of moving on myself."

"Up to the colony?" Elspeth asked, her face lighting up.

"I was thinking of going west. This place is changing so fast—all these people moving in."

"But that's just why you're needed!" said Elspeth earnestly. "People like Mrs. Galbraith need you."

"We're both better at giving advice than taking it," Dr. Wallace answered, smiling. "But I'll think about

what you've said. If I went up to the colony, and
things didn't work out for you with the Galbraiths, I
could give you a job as a maid. I'm sure Kate Morgan
would furnish you with a good reference!"

"I don't have to go with the Galbraiths," Elspeth
said. "I could work for you now!"

Dr. Wallace was taken aback by Elspeth's eagerness. He had spoken lightly, yet he did have a feeling
of responsibility for the child. All the same, he wasn't
sure that he wanted Elspeth under his own roof as a
constant reminder of his daughter, Megan. "You go
with the Galbraiths, lass," he said gently. "I imagine
that if I do go up to the colony, I'd be living in a tent
for the summer. A maid to answer the door might be
a bit pretentious!"

Elspeth smiled, then became serious again. "If you
leave here, who'll let me know if Robbie comes
back?"

"You could ask Mrs. Morgan," Dr. Wallace suggested. "But you shouldn't go on expecting him—not
after so long. . . ." Dr. Wallace stopped abruptly. It
*was* easier to give advice than to take it.

Elspeth's face had lost all its animation. Picking up
a tray of dirty dishes, she went through to the
kitchen, her gray eyes blank and defeated, her face
pinched and thin.

Mrs. Galbraith and the twins had been in the hotel
in Battleford for a week when John Galbraith came
down from the colony. Matthew had stayed up on
the claim to take care of the animals, so Mr. Galbraith
was anxious to get started on the return trip without

any unnecessary delay. The girls, who had been beside themselves with excitement at the prospect of seeing their father again after two months, were subdued and shy when he actually came. He teased them about their short hair, and they stood there, shuffling, eyes downcast, with nothing to say. But when he began to tell their mother about the house and the sod barn and the new animals, they interrupted with a stream of questions. Rachel suddenly blurted out that Elspeth was going to live with them.

"That was something I planned to talk to you about, John," Molly Galbraith said. "She's on her own, poor lass, and she'd be a help with the housework and the children."

"I don't know where we'll put her," Mr. Galbraith answered doubtfully. "And we can't pay her much in wages, with what I've already spent on lumber and animals. But if you think she'd be a help to you. . . ."

When Elspeth told Mrs. Morgan that she was going up to the colony with the Galbraiths, she was quite unprepared for the outburst of anger that greeted the news.

"After all I've done for you!" Mrs. Morgan raged. "Downright deceitful, I call it—going off and getting another job like that."

"But I thought—I thought you were just letting me stay here. I wasn't getting paid—"

"I treated you like my own daughter! I gave you a home. I even gave you the dress you're wearing."

So Elspeth couldn't ask the angry Mrs. Morgan to let her know if she ever heard anything about

Robbie. She went up to the bare back bedroom to bundle up her blankets and pack her few clothes. She wondered about giving Mrs. Morgan back the green dress, but she couldn't bear the thought of wearing her old dress again and shoved it into the traveling bag. In the bottom of the bag, wrapped in a piece of soft flannel, she still had Mama's cairngorm brooch and Papa's watch. With no money, she knew that the day might come when she would have to sell these to buy new clothes. In the other side of the traveling bag were Robbie's clothes—his extra socks, his under-wear and trousers, and a small, ragged blue jersey. She wondered if she should leave them behind. But she was going to find Robbie up there in the colony, and he'd be needing his extra clothes! That was the best reason of all for going with Rachel and Rebecca —so that she could look for Robbie herself. She snapped the traveling bag closed and ran downstairs to join the Galbraiths.

Pulling aside the net curtain on the dining-room window, Mrs. Morgan watched Elspeth leave. She was vexed because she really didn't want the girl to go. At first she had resented the way Dr. Wallace had insisted that she provide Elspeth with a place to stay. She had thought her too sickly and plain ever to be any use around the hotel. But Elspeth had worked hard, and today, going off with these well-dressed English people in their fancy democrat wagon, she looked almost pretty. She had lost that dull, with-drawn look that annoyed Mrs. Morgan. "So that's all the thanks I get, after all I've done for her!" Mrs.

Morgan muttered, letting the net curtain fall back into place.

Only a few days after Elspeth left, two men came to the hotel, and each of them asked about Elspeth. Both times, out of sheer spite, Mrs. Morgan said that she had no idea where Elspeth was. She didn't tell either of them that Elspeth had worked there until very recently.

The first man was Scottish, and Mrs. Morgan wondered if he might be the uncle that Elspeth had talked so much about when she was ill. He didn't seem terribly interested in finding the girl. When Mrs. Morgan said she didn't know where Elspeth was, he accepted that and left.

The second man was more persistent. An English lad, and in spite of his working clothes, Mrs. Morgan could tell he was a gentleman. The kind of person she liked to have stay in the hotel. She would have been friendlier if he had booked a room, but he said he had no money for that.

"How long did Elspeth stay here?" he asked.

"With all the people who put up here, how do you expect me to remember one girl?"

"She was ill while she was here—you must remember her. And Dr. Wallace said she worked here."

"When did he tell you that?" Mrs. Morgan asked.

"Back in May. I had hoped to see him here—I wanted to tell him about the land I've got—but they say he's gone back up to Headquarters Camp. But, about Elspeth. . . ."

"I know the girl you mean. I just don't remember how long she was here. Maybe a week or two."

"Was her little brother ever found?"

"I never believed there was one! That girl told a pack of lies, that I do remember!"

"She had a brother, all right. I knew them both. I'll leave my name. Maybe, if you ever hear anything of Elspeth, you could get in touch with me," he said, handing her a scrap of paper.

She glanced at the name—*Arthur Whitcomb*—and then dropped the paper into a drawer in the hall table.

# 13

## "The wealth of the land"

### JULY

THE THREE-DAY JOURNEY FROM BATTLEFORD UP TO the claim was pleasant and uneventful. Because of the warm weather, the marshy places on the trail had dried out and the streams were easy to ford. Along the route the government had established stopping places with tents and firewood, and so the Galbraiths spent their nights in relative comfort. But they were still very glad to reach the end of their journey.

All the way from Battleford John Galbraith talked proudly about the new house. He had bought a load of logs and had hired a man to help him with the building, because he wanted the house built right so that it would withstand the cold of winter. The walls were chinked with mud, and under the floor, which was made from smooth boards from the sawmill, was a root cellar. Molly Galbraith must have expected something bigger and grander than a small log cabin with a sod roof. But if she compared it in her mind to their tall, ivy-covered house in Carlisle, with its bay windows and wrought-iron railings and rose garden, she said nothing.

While Mr. Galbraith was helping the twins down

from the wagon, Matthew came out of the barn. He stopped short when he saw the girls and asked, "What happened to your hair? Did the Indians get you? I warned you that they liked red pigtails!"

Elspeth watched him from behind the wagon, feeling awkward about seeing him again. She remembered how he had made her angry on the boat by bragging that he could get a job on a farm, but she could see now that he had spoken the truth. Dressed in overalls, cap, and boots, he looked more a man than a boy, striding up from the barn.

"Elspeth's going to stay with us!" Rachel shouted to him, eager to beat Rebecca with the news. "And she's lost Robbie!"

"Lost Robbie!" Matthew repeated. Then, seeing Elspeth standing beside the wagon, he asked, "What are you doing here? I thought you were going to Manitoba."

"I want to see the house," Mrs. Galbraith said quickly, trying to divert attention from Elspeth, who was close to tears. "Everything else must wait!"

The house was divided into three rooms—two small bedrooms on one side and the kitchen-living room on the other. Because the rooms were sparsely furnished, they seemed quite big.

"We'll move you into the kitchen, Matthew," his father said. "Then the girls can have the bedroom."

"Putting up curtains will help," Mrs. Galbraith said, looking around. "And maybe you could make some shelves for the dishes, John. It will be good to unpack our things at last."

Matthew had a pot of stew simmering on the fire, and they were soon seated around the table.

"I think this is the first time we have all eaten together since we left England," Mrs. Galbraith said, smiling at them. "And that seems so long ago!"

Elspeth looked at their happy faces. Perhaps it had been a mistake to come. She ached for her own family—for Mama and Papa and Robbie. Especially for Robbie. That night, she lay on a straw mattress next to the twins, listening to their even breathing, and tears ran down her cheeks. Not knowing if Robbie was safe made it harder for her to live in the friendly atmosphere of the Galbraith family.

The following day, Mrs. Galbraith unpacked boxes of material, laces, buttons, and thread. "We had a draper's shop in Carlisle," she explained to Elspeth. "Before we sold it, I packed away some things I thought we might need."

"It must have been lovely to have all this in your own shop," Elspeth said. "Aren't you going to miss it?"

"Yes," said Mrs. Galbraith with a sigh. "But John's happier here. He never really did enjoy listening to women decide whether to make their summer dresses from purple-sprigged muslin or yellow silk! I miss the aunties, too. They lived with us in Carlisle, but they said they were too old to start a new life here. There's a lot of things to weigh one against the other when you take a step like we did, and you're still left wondering if you did right."

The girls helped Mrs. Galbraith stitch curtains out

of crisp white cotton. While Elspeth sewed, she thought about Mrs. Galbraith's words. For her there hadn't been many choices—only one. After that, everything else had followed. Yet she, too, wondered if she'd done right. But she'd find Robbie! Here in the colony she'd have more chance to look for him.

Before Mrs. Galbraith put away the boxes, she let the girls pick out material for dresses she would make over the winter. Elspeth fingered some soft red wool material, wondering if Mrs. Galbraith meant her to choose too.

"That would look nice on you, Elspeth," Mrs. Galbraith said, lifting out the red material. "With maybe a touch of lace on the collar and cuffs."

The long summer days were filled with hard work. The girls brought in water from the spring and helped wash the clothes and peg them on the line. They swept the floors—a futile task, Elspeth thought, with people tracking dirt in all the time. They also kept an eye on the two cows grazing on the lush grass behind the barn, and brought them in for milking in the evening. Elspeth mostly let the twins look after the cows because Buttercup was going to have a calf soon, and that reminded her too sharply of Robbie.

Mr. Galbraith had planted several acres of potatoes and turnips, and also a field of oats for winter fodder for the animals. It was too late in the season to plant wheat, their main money crop, but he was already getting the ground ready for next year. He and Matthew had plowed and harrowed ten acres. The soil was rich enough, but it was full of stones. He set the girls to gather them.

Matthew had made a stone-boat, which consisted of boards nailed to log runners. The girls walked over the plowed ground gathering rocks, and piled them on the stone-boat. When it was full, Matthew would harness Bessie to it and drag the stones away, piling them at the edge of the field. The pile of stones grew bigger, but the number in the field never seemed to grow any less.

"The raspberries over by the bluff are ripe," Elspeth told Mrs. Galbraith eagerly. "Would you like us to pick some for jam?" The girls much preferred picking raspberries, or strawberries, or the small, tart saskatoon berries, to gathering stones. They also enjoyed turning over the sweet-smelling, new-mown hay.

Mrs. Galbraith made bonnets for Elspeth and the twins, to protect them from the strong sun. She scolded Rachel and Rebecca when they didn't wear them. "You'll get sunstroke, with your hair so short," she warned them. "And your faces will be covered with freckles!"

Actually, their hair was getting thick again, but it was true about the freckles. Elspeth, whose bonnet also dangled down her back, looked brown and healthy. Dr. Wallace would have been pleased to see her.

As the time for the baby's birth drew closer, Mrs. Galbraith became more and more worried and depressed. The twins' birth had not been easy. This time she had already suffered a great deal of sickness. They were farther from the town site than she had expected, and she had no neighbors to call on for help.

One morning, Mr. Galbraith called Matthew and the girls together, saying, "I'm going to take your ma down to the town site. I'm hoping that Mrs. Lloyd, the minister's wife, will know of somewhere she can stay till after this baby's born. I'm not planning on getting back myself until at least the day after tomorrow, but you've managed the animals on your own before, Matthew. This time you'll have the girls to help you."

The girls watched Mr. and Mrs. Galbraith drive away in the democrat wagon pulled by Bessie and Daisy.

"No rocks today!" Rachel said, jumping up and down with excitement.

"Nor tomorrow either!" said Rebecca.

"You've still to do your work," Matthew said sternly.

"But Bessie's not here to pull the stone-boat," Rebecca pointed out quickly. "Unless you're going to pull it yourself!"

"There's other things you can do," Matthew said gruffly.

That was true, but it was hard for them to settle to their usual tasks with Mama gone and the house so quiet. Even Matthew found that. After lunch, he said he thought he would go down to the slough to cut firewood. Rachel wanted to go with him, until she remembered how bad the mosquitoes were there.

"We'll go and pick raspberries," Elspeth suggested. "But we should fetch water first."

The afternoon passed quickly. Supper, with fresh raspberries for dessert, tasted good. It was later than usual when Matthew went out to milk Buttercup and Marigold, only to find that they had strayed from the patch of grass behind the barn.

"You're supposed to watch them," Matthew told the twins.

"We couldn't watch them *and* pick raspberries," Rebecca said.

"They'll be over by the bluff, I expect," Matthew said. "They seem to think the grass is better over there. Come and help me fetch them, Rachel."

About fifteen minutes after Matthew and Rachel left, there was a sudden loud knock at the door. The Galbraiths' house was not near any traveled trail, and with so few people in the area, they never had unexpected visitors. Elspeth and Rebecca stared at one another in surprise and made no move to answer the door. The knock was repeated, loudly, urgently.

Elspeth opened the door cautiously. A man stood leaning against the door frame, sweat beading his pale forehead.

"May I come in?" he asked, stumbling forward into the room. "And can you do something about my horse? Hide it! They'll see it and know I'm here."

Elspeth looked at the man—his lined face, round glasses, and white cap. It was Mr. Barr! Isaac Moses

Barr, the man she had so badly wanted to find. But that had been long ago, while she still had Robbie with her.

"Mr. Barr, sir!" she said. "Whatever brings you here?"

"Can you hide the horse?" he asked. "They'll see it."

Elspeth didn't wait to ask any of the questions crowding her brain. She fetched a mug of water from the pail by the door, handed it to Mr. Barr, and then told Rebecca to come with her. She went outside and led the horse over to the barn, tethering it in Bessie's empty stall.

"Get some oats and a bucket of water, Rebecca. I'll take the saddle off and brush it down. It's been ridden hard, poor thing."

Elspeth had watched Arthur and Sidney working with the horses on the way from Saskatoon, but watching was different from doing it herself. However, Mr. Barr's horse was either too docile or too exhausted to protest at Elspeth's lack of skill.

When the girls crossed back from the sod barn to the house they saw, to their astonishment, that they were about to have more company. Three riders were galloping over the prairie toward their house from the direction of the town site.

Isaac Barr, who was pacing the floor in his agitation, swung around when they came in and asked, "Did you find somewhere to hide it?"

"There's no place to hide a horse here, Mr. Barr.

I've put it in Bessie's stall. There's three men coming this way now, but maybe they'll think the horse is ours."

"Is there anywhere I can hide?"

"The root cellar," said Rebecca immediately, struggling to move two heavy floorboards. Her eyes were dancing with excitement. "We won't tell *them* you're here."

Unceremoniously, they shoved Mr. Barr down into the cellar.

"Crawl farther in—it's deeper farther back," Elspeth advised him.

They had just got the boards back in place and moved the table slightly to hide the crack when someone began to pound on the door.

"Remember! Shadow Bairns are quiet," Elspeth said softly to Rebecca, just before opening the door.

"We're looking for Barr," one of the men said, pushing his way into the house. "Have you seen anyone ride past here?"

"Barr?" Elspeth repeated. "Would that be the Mr. Barr who started the colony?"

"That's the man we mean. Though Barabbas would be a better name for him than Barr."

"Not many people come this way," Elspeth said. "We would surely have seen him if he had."

"Are you girls alone?"

"My big brother, Matthew, is getting the cows," Rebecca answered.

"Why would you be wanting Mr. Barr?" Elspeth

asked innocently, as if she were in no hurry to get rid of these rough strangers.

"Why would we not be wanting him?" one of them said with a harsh laugh.

"It's a little matter of justice," said another. "We filed for land on the boat, and now it turns out that the railroad is going through that parcel of land. And whose name is it in? Isaac Barr's!"

"But surely there's plenty of land for everyone," said Elspeth.

"The land the railroad passes through is going to be valuable. Why should he make a profit on land that was rightfully ours?" the man asked angrily.

"You're wasting time, Fred," the third man broke in. "We'd better take a look around the place and see that he's not skulking about it. These children are on their own."

Elspeth actually felt more comfortable with Mr. Barr than with the three ruffians who were looking for him in the name of justice. She watched helplessly while two of the men went out to search the barn. The other searched the house. It didn't take him long, for there were very few places to hide in the cabin.

The two men soon came back, apparently accepting that the only horse in the barn belonged there. But Elspeth's relief was short-lived. From the small front window she could see Matthew and Rachel making their slow way up from the bluff, leading Marigold and Buttercup. Matthew wouldn't overlook a strange horse in Bessie's stall, eating Bessie's oats. Elspeth wondered if it would make the men suspicious if she ran out and intercepted Matthew so that she could tell him about Mr. Barr hiding in their root cellar, but she dismissed the idea. Matthew never had been sympathetic toward Barr.

Matthew stopped mid-stride as he noticed the horses tethered by the door. He said something to Rachel and gave her Buttercup's rope. He came straight over to the house, and Rachel disappeared, leading both cows to the barn.

Matthew heard the men out and then said curtly, "We haven't seen Isaac Barr around here, and that suits me. So you'd better be on your way. You're losing time."

"Can you spare us something to eat?" one of the men asked. "If we're heading out toward Battleford, I'd sooner have supper first."

"I can give you some bread and corned beef," Elspeth said. "But you'd better take it with you. You don't want to be wasting any more time."

But it was too late. Elspeth could hear Rachel running toward the house, eager to share the news that there was a strange horse in Bessie's stall. If there was some way to make her be quiet!

It was Rebecca who knew the way. Just as the door opened, and before Rachel had a chance to speak, Rebecca called out, "Rachel, *they* have come! *They* are looking for Mr. Barr."

Rachel caught Rebecca's eye, and a flicker of understanding passed between them.

"*They* are looking for Mr. Barr," she repeated in a low voice.

Don't overdo it, Elspeth pleaded to herself. But the men were diverted by the sudden appearance of a second little girl exactly like the first.

"We'd better stay off the bottle," one of the men joked. "I'm seeing double!"

"Was Mr. Barr on horseback?" Rachel asked, and the men forgot their jokes and turned their full attention on the child. Elspeth felt sick and reached for the back of a chair to support herself.

"When we were looking for the cows, I saw a man riding over that way in the next section."

"When was this?" one man asked.

"How fast was he going?" asked another.

"Maybe an hour ago. Maybe not so long. I thought his horse seemed tired."

"Give us the food and we'll be on our way!"

Elspeth hoped they wouldn't notice her shaking hands as she gave them the bread and some corned beef they could ill spare. Matthew followed them to the door, saying that he was going out to do the milking. He watched them mount and ride off to the east.

"Matthew, don't go yet," Elspeth begged. "Just wait a few minutes longer."

"Whatever for?"

"I'd rather not be in the house alone until those men are well out of sight."

"Don't be daft! They've gone. They won't be back."

"Are you going to tell him about the horse now?" Rachel asked, bursting with curiosity.

"What horse?" Matthew asked.

"The one in our barn."

By the time Matthew understood that Isaac Barr was actually hiding under their floor, and that his horse was calmly eating oats in the barn, the men were already too far away to call back. Which was just as well, because that was exactly what Matthew wanted to do. But he admitted that he didn't trust the three men looking for Barr any more than he trusted Barr himself.

"It's just as well they didn't meet here," he said seriously. "Did you notice that one of the men had a gun? They mean business."

When Isaac Barr crawled out from the root cellar, his glasses crooked and his clothes covered with earth and dirt, he looked more shaken than ever. He had overheard most of what had been said. He had been waiting to be found at any moment, trapped in his hole like a rabbit by a stoat. He was embarrassingly grateful to the children, calling them blessed in the eyes of the Lord.

Elspeth tried to stop his flow of words by asking, "What will you do now?"

"I am turning my back on my people," he said. "For they have turned against me. I led them to the Promised Land, and now no one listens to me. They have chosen George Exton Lloyd to lead them. They cannot see that I took risks too, and should be rewarded. Am I not entitled to some profit from this enterprise? Am I supposed to turn everything over to them, when it was I who had the vision that made the whole venture possible?"

"But what are you going to do now?" Elspeth asked.

"I'll wait here for a bit, if I may," Mr. Barr said, suddenly forgetting his pulpit voice. "When it gets dark, I'll try and get down to Battleford. I still have a few friends there I can trust."

"It's like playing Shadow Bairns, only it's real," Rebecca said. "Riding through the dark with *them* looking for you."

"So you know about Shadow Bairns too," Mr. Barr said to Rebecca in surprise.

"How do *you* know about them?" Elspeth broke in.

"A little boy told me, just a week or two ago. He thought that I was one of *them*."

"A little boy with curly blond hair?" Elspeth asked in a breathless whisper. "About four years old?"

"That's the lad!" answered Isaac Barr. "His name is Robbie."

# 14

## "Success"

JULY 29–30

THERE WAS A MOMENT OF COMPLETE SILENCE AS Elspeth, Matthew, and the twins grasped the meaning of Mr. Barr's words. Robbie was alive. Mr. Barr had seen him. They were close to finding him at last.

"Where is he, Mr. Barr?" Elspeth asked breathlessly. "He's my little brother. I lost him three months ago."

"He's with some people who have a quarter section down on the south boundary of the colony. Good land, they've got."

"Who are they? What's their name?"

"Beattie. Jim and Janet Beattie."

Mrs. Beattie! Elspeth closed her eyes and was suddenly back in her dream in the hotel room in Battleford. Her limbs were heavy, her bones aching, Robbie's crying voice was right inside her skull. "I'm hungry, Elspeth! Talk to me!" Then there had been another voice—a flat, insistent voice. "We'll take the wee lad with us. You're in no state to cope. The land agent will tell you where we've settled. Do you understand? Check with the land agent." Elspeth had opened her eyes and seen the shadows of two figures on the wall across the room. Two distorted shadows —a small boy and a tall woman—the tall shadow reaching up to the roof and bent sharply across the ceiling. It had grown bigger and bigger until the whole room had turned dark and then she slept again. Mrs. Beattie had taken Robbie and had told her where to find him.

Isaac Barr was still talking. "Now that I think about it, they said something about the lad not being theirs. Their own son died of diphtheria in Scotland a year ago, so they decided to leave there, with all its sad associations, and start over again in a new land."

"So they stole Robbie because they'd lost their own boy," Matthew said.

"I don't think that's the way of it," Mr. Barr said. "They spoke quite openly about him not being their son."

"To you, maybe, but not to Dr. Wallace," Elspeth said. "Mrs. Beattie didn't tell Dr. Wallace that Robbie was there when he asked her."

"We can worry about that later," Matthew said. "What we have to do now is find out exactly where the Beatties' section is so that we can get Robbie back."

"If it's south of here, you could take me there, Mr. Barr," Elspeth said eagerly. "You're going that way, and you know where it is."

"Don't be silly!" Matthew broke in impatiently. "You can't go with him, not when armed men are looking for him. You don't want to get mixed up in that. And he isn't going to shorten the odds of escaping by taking you along to find Robbie. Wait till Pa gets home."

"When will that be?" Elspeth asked. "Do you think I can wait two days, three days, not knowing for certain?"

"You've waited all summer," Matthew pointed out.

"But it's different now! I know where to look."

"She's right, Matthew," Rebecca said. "She can't wait any more days now."

"They are looking after the boy well," Mr. Barr said. "The Beatties are good, God-fearing people."

"Mr. Barr, sir," Elspeth said, crossing the room and standing directly in front of him. "All the way here, even when things were really bad, like in the Immigration Building in Saskatoon, I always knew that if I could just find you, you would help me. You see, I remembered you saying on the boat how you were responsible for us, for all of us, and I knew then you'd help me. And I was right! You've told me where Robbie is, when no one else helped. So, please, take me there. You don't need to stop or anything—just show me the way."

Elspeth could have reminded Barr that he owed her his life, but she didn't even think of that. Perhaps it was just as well. Barr didn't have much of a record for honoring bargains.

Instead, her words recalled the high hopes he once

had for all these people he was leading to a better
land. He squared his shoulders, and a little color
crept back into his ashen face. "I'll take you to find
your young brother," he said steadily. "But maybe I
could rest somewhere for a few hours first and have a
bite to eat. If we leave around midnight, we'll reach
the Beatties' place by dawn."

He slept in the Galbraith's bedroom. While he
slept, Matthew argued with Elspeth, telling her that
she was a fool to go with him, trying to persuade her
not to go.

"He's only taking you for his own safety," Matthew said. "He thinks those men won't shoot if he has
a girl along with him. You're nothing better than a
hostage. And they're liable to shoot first and be sorry
afterward."

"They're miles from here by now," Elspeth argued. "Anyway, they went east, not south."

"You can't trust Isaac Barr, Elspeth! Robbie may
not even be there."

"Don't you see, that's why I *have* to go!" Elspeth
said. "I can't rest until I find out."

"Then let *me* go," Matthew suggested.

"But *I* still wouldn't know if Rob was there,"
Elspeth pointed out. "It might be days before you got
back. This is something I have to do myself."

In the end, Matthew gave in. He stood in the
doorway, in the early hours of the morning, and
watched Barr ride away with Elspeth behind him,
clinging to his broad back. As they were swallowed

up in the darkness, he thought that, even with armed men lurking out there, Elspeth was lucky to be going. It was worse staying at home, waiting.

During the rough ride, Elspeth's thoughts were centered entirely on Robbie. The howl of the coyote, the looming shapes of stunted bushes, the pattern of light and shadow in the moonlight, all went unnoticed. Her biggest fear was that Rob would not be there, that her hopes had been raised only to be smashed again. She knew she couldn't stand that. *Please, please make Robbie be there.* The words drummed through her mind to the beat of the horse's hoofs, eating up the miles, bringing her nearer the truth. *Please, please make Robbie be there.*

Elspeth had lost all track of time when the sun at last came up over the horizon, bringing with it the promise of another hot day. They could see for miles in every direction. Mr. Barr seemed more relaxed, perhaps because riding in daylight was easier than it had been in the darkness.

He reined in the horse and spoke to Elspeth over his shoulder. "I had thought of stopping in and asking Jim Beattie if he would lend me another horse, but it's sometimes hard to know who your friends are these days, so I'll just go on past the bluff and rest. That means I leave you here. You can see their house behind that clump of cottonwoods about a mile away. The trail west leads right to it."

Mr. Barr dismounted and helped Elspeth down. He seemed reluctant to leave. He was facing the sun, and the light was catching the thick lenses of his glasses.

"It's people like you that this land needs," he said. "Young, adaptable, willing to learn. Do something worthwhile, lass, and I'll have a part in it too. Make a place for yourself here."

"Thank you, Mr. Barr. I'll do that," Elspeth said quietly, her eyes brimming with tears. No matter what people said about Mr. Barr, Elspeth knew he had not failed. He had a part in everything the settlers did here, because it had been his dream.

Mr. Barr mounted his horse clumsily and rode away. Elspeth, stiff from the long ride, walked slowly down the trail that led to the Beatties' house. Her heart was pounding and her mouth dry. Now that she was so close there was no need to hurry. If Robbie was there, he was likely still asleep. If he wasn't there, then she'd as soon not know.

The house wasn't like the rough log or sod cabins that most of the settlers had built. It was made of smooth boards and had a shingle roof. A good house, with glass windows in painted frames. Lace curtains. Smoke was curling from the chimney. Someone must be up already. Elspeth covered the last few yards to the door, raised her hand, and knocked.

The door was opened immediately by Mrs. Beattie. The expression on her passive face changed a fraction when she saw Elspeth standing there. "So you've come at last," she said. "You'd better come inside."

Elspeth followed the woman into the room. The picture of Mrs. Beattie insisting that if one stick of her furniture was left behind, then she would stay too, came sharply to Elspeth's mind. It had paid off. The room was well furnished with pictures on the wall, a painted china oil lamp on a small cane table, and a sewing box on another table. Near it lay a pair of boy's patched trousers.

And then Elspeth saw, lying carelessly on a shelf, scrubbed clean and with the missing eyes replaced—Pig-Bear! Running across the room, she picked it up and clutched it to her. Turning around, she asked, "Where is he? Where is Robbie?"

"Why have you been so long in coming?" Mrs. Beattie asked. "We thought you weren't coming at all."

"I didn't know where to come."

"The land agent would have told you. I said so the night we found Robbie crying in the hotel."

"But I didn't understand. I was sick, you see."

"I knew that. I told that girl Peg that we would look after Robbie till you were better. I told her to get you into your nightgown and fetch the doctor. You needed more care than I could have given you."

"She got me into a nightgown," Elspeth said bitterly. "And then she took off with my skirt and the money I had sewn into the bodice, though no one believes me. And she never called the doctor. It was the next day before Mrs. Morgan found me and fetched Dr. Wallace."

"She never called the doctor?" Mrs. Beattie said in

dismay. "And you so sick! Maybe we should have done more ourselves, but we were anxious to get to the colony. I never thought of you not knowing we had Robbie."

"But when I didn't come to find him, didn't you wonder then?"

"Aye. I wondered if maybe you just found it easier being on your own. It always seemed a big responsibility for you, so young yourself, having to look after the wee lad. And then we heard that your aunt and uncle were in Manitoba, so it never made sense them meeting you in Battleford, and that you had a job in the hotel."

"Dr. Wallace told you that, didn't he?" Elspeth said accusingly. "Why didn't you tell *him* you had Robbie. He was here, and you said you didn't know anything about Rob."

"Dr. Wallace?" Mrs. Beattie seemed puzzled for a moment. Then she said, "The man who came the day Jim was buying lumber for the house! I never knew he was a doctor. He never said, and I took him for an immigration official, the way he questioned me about the lad. I wasn't going to hand Robbie over to one of *them*. The boy's scared of these immigration people —of most strangers, for that matter! He calls himself a Shadow Bairn and hides from *them*. I thought he was getting over it, but Isaac Barr was here a week or two back, and Rob was as bad as ever."

"It was Mr. Barr who told me Robbie was here," Elspeth said. "Can I see him now? Is he sleeping?"

"He's already out at the barn helping Jim with the milking. He loves the animals. Go on out and see him."

Elspeth ran out of the house, over to the barn, her heart pounding with excitement. It took a moment for her eyes to adjust to the dim light inside the barn, and then she saw him. He was trying to coax a calf to drink milk from a pail. As he looked up, Elspeth saw his small face tense. The pail clattered to the ground, and he drew back into one of the stalls.

"It's me, Robbie! It's Elspeth!"

Cautiously, he peered around the end of the stall, his eyes huge and black in the dim light.

"Don't you know me, Robbie?" Elspeth asked, trying to keep her voice from rising. "Say something, Robbie! Tell me you're glad to see me!"

Then he was in her arms, burying his face in her dress, clinging to her.

"Come out in the light where I can get a look at you!"

He had been well cared for, she could see that. His hair had been trimmed, and he was wearing new boots and trousers.

"I thought you were never coming," he said, clinging to her again. "I thought you'd gone away, like Mama and Papa."

Then he smiled at her, his old impish smile, yet he didn't look quite the same. He was tidier and bigger, but it wasn't that. There was some change in him that she couldn't put her finger on.

"Do you want to see the calves, Elspeth?" Robbie

asked. "I have a calf of my own now—I call her Elspeth. Do you remember how I was going to call her Jock?"

Elspeth's eyes filled with tears. So Robbie had memories too. But what was it Papa had said—that Robbie accepted what happened and made the best of it.

She watched as he brought a black and white calf out of its stall. It butted him, nearly bowling him over, but he managed to guide it to Elspeth. "Let her lick your hand, Elspeth. Her tongue feels funny!"

Elspeth could hear the Beatties' voices outside. She turned around as Mr. Beattie came into the barn.

"The boy must be right pleased to see you," he said. "He wondered why you didn't come. We all did. I went down to the hotel, you know, but the woman didn't seem to remember you."

"But I worked there," Elspeth said. "I worked for Mrs. Morgan for nearly two months."

"It was just a week or two ago I was down there. There was always so much to do here, and all the time we were expecting you to come. When you didn't, I finally went down to Battleford to see what had happened to you."

"I suppose I had moved up with the Galbraiths by then, but Mrs. Morgan knew that. She could have told you."

"Aye. She wasn't a very talkative woman."

"Spiteful's more the word," said Elspeth.

"Well, it's good you found us. What will you be doing now?"

What would she do now? Elspeth realized that she hadn't thought beyond this moment of finding Robbie. The Galbraiths wouldn't have room for Robbie as well as her, not with the new baby. She didn't have money to pay their way to Manitoba, even if she wanted to go. She looked helplessly at Jim Beattie.

"It will break Janet's heart if you take the lad," he said slowly. "Our own boy, James, died a bit over a year ago, and she never really got over it. Not till she got to looking after your Robbie."

Elspeth said nothing. It was almost as if *they* had got Robbie after all. The Beatties were trying to take him away from her, to make him into their child.

"It's good to have him here," Jim continued in a low voice. "He's got farming in his blood, that boy. You should see him with the animals. It gives more future to this beginning we're making. Building a farm out of nothing is a slow business. A man needs someone to come after him. But let's go up to the house and have breakfast. You'll be hungry after that long ride."

It was strange to see Robbie so much at home with the Beatties. He left his boots by the door and hung his jacket on a low peg without being told. He helped himself to a bowl of porridge from the pot by the fire, and bowed his head when Jim Beattie asked the blessing before they ate.

After breakfast, Mrs. Beattie said to Elspeth, "If you've been up most of the night, you should have some sleep. What about these people you're staying

with now—the Galbraiths? How are they expecting
you to get back? It seems funny, them letting you
come on your own with Isaac Barr."

"They don't know I'm here," Elspeth answered.
"You see, Mr. Galbraith took his wife to the town site
because she's having a baby any day, and she wanted
to be close to the doctor."

"You came without telling anyone?"

"Matthew—their son—and Rachel and Rebecca
know."

"They played Shadow Bairns," said Robbie. "I
want to see Rachel and Rebecca."

"You do take things into your own hands, don't
you?" said Mrs. Beattie severely. "It seems you never
think before you act."

"But I couldn't wait for them to get back!" said
Elspeth. "I had to find Robbie, to make sure he was
here. It was awful not knowing where he was."

"Aye. That was bad, you not knowing for so long,"
said Mrs. Beattie. But there was no hint in her voice
or expression that she really understood how it had
been.

Lying on the Beatties' bed, trying to sleep, Elspeth
thought about Mrs. Beattie's words. It was true that
she acted first and thought afterward. Papa had said
that she bent things to suit herself. But this time she'd
plan it out properly. She'd get Robbie away from
here because the Beatties were trying to turn him
into their own son, and they had no claim on him. If
only she still had her money, they could go somewhere. The first thing to do was to find Peg and get

the money back. Failing that, she could sell Mama's brooch and Papa's watch. Then she would take Rob and they would go—where? Suddenly Isaac Barr's parting words came back to her. "Do something worthwhile, lass, and I'll have part in it, too. Make a place for yourself here." Of course, he was talking about the colony, not the Beatties' place.

Later in the day, following Robbie around the farm, Elspeth made a discovery that surprised and even troubled her a little. Robbie was happy with the Beatties. He loved everything about the farm. The dog, Paddy, belonged to him, and he seemed to belong to the dog. When he and Jim walked down to the barn together, Robbie stretched his short legs to match his stride to Jim's. He sometimes even forgot and called him Pa, and Mrs. Beattie's brusqueness didn't bother him at all. Now that Elspeth was here, his world was complete.

That evening, at the dinner table, Mr. Beattie said that he planned to ride to the town site the next day because there were a few supplies they needed, and he would see if John Galbraith was still there so that he could let him know where Elspeth was. "Even if I don't see him, I should be able to get a message to his wife. Do you want me to say you'll be coming back? I expect they'll be needing you with the new bairn."

"I don't know about going back there," Elspeth said slowly. "You see, they wouldn't have room for Robbie."

"But the lad's fine here," Mrs. Beattie said quickly.

"He's made himself right at home, and we like having him."

"But we are to stay together," Elspeth said. "I promised Mama. Maybe if you could just keep him till I get in touch with Uncle Donald."

"I don't want to find Uncle Donald," Robbie said, fighting back tears. "I don't want to be a Shadow Bairn again. I want to stay here. Why can't you stay too, Elspeth?"

"We'd be glad to have you, lass," Jim Beattie said quietly.

"It would seem to be the best answer all round," Mrs. Beattie said matter-of-factly.

Elspeth looked at the three faces watching her: Robbie's, tense and flushed; Mr. Beattie's, kind and understanding; and Mrs. Beattie's, strong and lined. Looking at Mrs. Beattie, Elspeth realized that some of the pain etched in the lines in her face and the sad, faraway look in her eyes had been caused by losing her boy. She could never get him back. She wasn't trying to fill his place with Robbie. No one could do that. She was just going on with life, reaching out a little—but not too far, in case she got hurt again— just as Elspeth had done at the Galbraiths'.

"I'd like to stay," said Elspeth. "But you're right that I have to go back to the Galbraiths' for a while. Mrs. Galbraith will need help with the new baby."

"But you'll stay here with Robbie for a few days first," Mrs. Beattie said firmly.

"Can I go with Elspeth, and see Rachel and Rebecca?" Robbie asked.

"You can ride along when I take Elspeth there," Mr. Beattie promised. "If we make an early start, we can visit for a while over lunch, and still get back for the evening chores."

Robbie nodded. "We'll be home in time for the milking," he said.

Papa had said these very words long ago when he and Elspeth went out in the boat to check the lobster pots, or up on the moor to cut peat. And he'd still used these words when they lived in Glasgow and there were no more cows to milk. Elspeth smiled at Robbie, though tears weren't far away. Threads of memory held them together as a family still. She was suddenly fiercely glad that *they* hadn't taken Robbie from her.

# 15

## "A picture that is highly rose-colored"

### JUNE, 1904

"NOTHING FOR YOU TODAY, MR. WHITCOMB," THE post mistress said. Noticing Arthur's disappointment, she added, "I expect there'll be a letter next time you're in."

Arthur shrugged. He walked out of Lloydminster post office and paused for a few minutes on the board sidewalk. Lloydminster was now a thriving community with two cafés, a butcher shop, a blacksmith's and two general stores. The school was nearly complete and plans were being made to build a church. The town had been named after George Exton Lloyd, who had taken over leadership of the colony. Isaac Moses Barr, whose dream had started it all, was almost forgotten.

In spite of the feeling of hope and excitement around him, Arthur felt let down. He had been hoping for news from his brother. Geoffrey couldn't stand the isolation of their cabin out there on the claim and had taken off last winter. Arthur had sometimes thought about giving up too, when the snow had lasted so long, and he saw no one for weeks on end. But he was glad now that he'd stuck it out.

All the same, he was in no hurry to head back out over the prairie to his small cabin that June morning.

Farther along the street, Arthur noticed a new doctor's surgery. On seeing the name on the sign, he stopped and went inside.

"Dr. Wallace," he said, shaking hands with the bearded doctor.

"It's Arthur Whitcomb, isn't it?" Dr. Wallace answered with a smile.

"That's right! And I owe you ten dollars. I'm living out on my own claim. It's good land I've got."

"That was a gift, not a loan," Dr. Wallace said gruffly. "I hear that your brother left early in the winter." The doctor heard most of what went on in the area.

"It was too quiet for him here," Arthur said. "He finally won some money at cards and took a train back east."

"And you'd have spent the money on a cow!" said the doctor. "But you must be lonely on your own."

"I was hoping for a letter today," Arthur confessed.

"It takes time for letters to get here, lad. You'll hear from him one of these days."

"By the way," Arthur said. "Do you know what happened to Elspeth and Robbie MacDonald? I went down to Battleford about a year ago, but Elspeth had left the hotel by then. Did she ever find Robbie?"

"Oh, yes! It was Barr, really, who helped her find him."

"Isaac Barr!"

"Elspeth had moved to the colony with the Galbraiths. While she was there, Barr came through. He told her that Robbie was with the Beatties down by the south boundary."

"Would that be Jim Beattie who traveled up from Saskatoon with us?"

"That's right. Now both Elspeth and Robbie are living there."

"But why did the Beatties take Robbie like that and let Elspeth think he was lost?" Arthur asked.

"It was more a misunderstanding, really."

"You say they're still living there?"

"Aye. The Galbraiths would have given Elspeth a home, but they didn't have much room. They had a new bairn last summer—Johnnie, a fine lad! One of the first to be born here in the colony."

"The MacDonald children are all right, are they? I've always felt a bit responsible." Arthur had only indistinct memories of the Beatties, but they seemed an unlikely couple to have given a home to Elspeth and Robbie.

"Jim Beattie's a good farmer," said Dr. Wallace. "They'll be fine there. How about you?"

"I'm not plowing many acres," Arthur admitted. "I need more capital first, so I'm still picking up work here and there. Do you think that Jim Beattie—?"

"I said he was a good farmer. I wouldn't be surprised but what he's breaking a lot of new land this year and will want help. You might even like working there," Dr. Wallace added, his blue eyes twinkling.

"Have you moved up here permanently?" Arthur asked, changing the subject.

"Aye," said the doctor. "There was a need for me here."

As Arthur was leaving, Dr. Wallace said, "If you do get a job with Jim Beattie, I'll likely see you. I usually stop in there when I have a call in that area. You can tell Elspeth I've written to Megan."

"Megan?" Arthur repeated.

"Elspeth will know!"

Elspeth was sitting at the kitchen table with a history book and an atlas open in front of her. School had closed for the summer, but Elspeth still studied whenever she had the chance. It was all part of her plan. She was learning all that she could, because someday she was going to be a teacher. There was a real need for teachers in the colony. Elspeth hadn't told anyone about her plan yet, but she liked to think about it. She didn't rush into things headlong now. This time she knew where she was going, and was content to wait for it to happen.

"How often do I need to ask you to clear away these books so I can set the table?" Mrs. Beattie asked.

Elspeth jumped guiltily. She didn't mean to annoy Mrs. Beattie, but they did get on each other's nerves sometimes. When she was a teacher, she would live in the schoolhouse with Robbie. Of course, it would be hard to get Robbie away from the farm. He was happy here with the Beatties.

"Don't stand there daydreaming, Elspeth! There's the pitcher and mugs to go on the table."

During supper there was a knock at the door. Elspeth glanced at Robbie and was glad to see that he didn't shrink away from the table the way he used to when someone came unexpectedly. He didn't worry about *them* now.

"See who it is, lass," Mrs. Beattie said briskly.

Elspeth opened the door and was completely taken aback to find Arthur Whitcomb standing there. The last time she had seen him had been in the hallway of the hotel in Battleford when her head had been swimming and her cheeks burning with fever. She felt her face grow warm now as Arthur just stood there, staring at her.

Arthur was wondering if this really could be Elspeth MacDonald. Could she have changed so much in one year? He had been expecting to see a thin-faced child in a ragged brown dress, with a little brother close beside her like a shadow. Instead, he found himself looking at a girl with golden lights in her hair and a red wool dress that showed off her slender figure. Her eyes were still the same—wide gray eyes with long, dark lashes.

"You're one of the Whitcomb lads," Mr. Beattie said, getting up from the table and shaking Arthur warmly by the hand.

"I'm Arthur."

"How are you and your brother making out?"

"Geoffrey left last winter. I've got a claim north-east of here, but I'm not doing much with it yet. I'm looking for work."

"I could use some help—from now through haying."

"Come and have supper with us," Mrs. Beattie said. "I'll set an extra place."

Arthur thanked Mrs. Beattie. He hardly recognized her as the same woman who had stared into the wind on the trail up from Saskatoon. She had lost that unseeing look.

Arthur sat down opposite Elspeth. Dr. Wallace was right, he was thinking. He *was* going to like working here. Elspeth stared down at her plate. Conversation became stiff and stilted, but then Arthur caught sight of Pig-Bear propped up on a shelf.

"That was my toy when I was little," Robbie explained seriously, and they all laughed.

"Do you remember the day Pig-Bear went swimming in Eagle Creek?" Arthur asked.

"And Elspeth!" Mrs. Beattie added, rather to Elspeth's annoyance.

Suddenly they were all sharing memories of the journey from Saskatoon to Battleford.

"And we thought that when we reached the colony, that would be the end of our troubles," Arthur said. "For most of us they were only beginning."

"Aye," said Mrs. Beattie. "But some of us got more than we expected when we read those high-flown words of Isaac Barr's!"

" 'I do not desire to present a picture that is highly rose-colored . . .' " Elspeth began, and then her eyes met Arthur's across the table. Suddenly there weren't enough words in all Barr's pamphlets to describe how wonderful the future was going to be.

# AUTHOR'S NOTE

ELSPETH AND ROBBIE, the orphaned children in this book, are my own invention but I have based the details of their journey on letters, diaries and other records written by the pioneers of that time. Of special value was a letter written by Arthur Black who came with Isaac Moses Barr to Canada in the year 1903. Elspeth's optimism and determination are characteristic of the Barr Colonists who sailed on *The Lake Manitoba* and settled the Saskatchewan Territory.

MARGARET J. ANDERSON is recognized as a storyteller of special gifts. "Anderson's simple, almost stark prose is most expressive," (*School Library Journal*.) "The author deftly weaves a plot around personal needs and relationships . . . She allows us to share her insight with a very special story bound to keep us in its spell." (*Language Arts*.) She is the author of *To Nowhere and Back*, an Outstanding Book of the Year (*New York Times Book Review*), *In the Keep of Time*, *In the Circle of Time*, and *Searching for Shona*, a nominee for The Dorothy Canfield Fisher Award.

She was born and educated in Scotland and graduated from the University of Edinburgh with honors in genetics. She now lives in Corvallis, Oregon with her husband and four children.